Dedalus Origin[al]

DEFYI[NG]

Karina Mellinger was born
French and Italian at Ox
England and Italy. In 1995 she gave up work to bring
sons up. She now writes full time.

Dedalus published her novel *A Bit Of A Marriage* to critical acclaim in 2006.

To Cazzer

The characters and situation in this work are wholly fictional and imaginary, and do not portray and are not intended to portray any actual persons or parties.

Karina Mellinger

Defying Reality

Dedalus

Published in the UK by Dedalus Ltd
Langford Lodge, St Judith's Lane, Sawtry, Cambs, PE28 5XE
email: info@dedalusbooks.com
www.dedalusbooks.com

ISBN 978 1 903517 61 1

Dedalus is distributed in the United States by SCB Distributors
15608 South New Century Drive, Gardena, California 90248
email: info@scbdistributors.com   web site: www.scbdistributors.com

Dedalus is distributed in Australia & New Zealand by Peribo Pty Ltd
58 Beaumont Road, Mount Kuring-gai N.S.W. 2080
email: peribo@bigpond.com

Dedalus is distributed in Canada by Disticor Direct-Book Division
695 Westney Road South, Suite 14 Ajax, Ontario, LI6 6M9
web site: www.disticordirect.com

First published by Dedalus in 2007

Defying Reality © copyright Karina Mellinger 2007

The right of Karina Mellinger to be identified as the author of this book has been asserted by her in accordance with the Copyright, Designs and Patent Acts, 1988.

Printed in Finland by WS Bookwell
Typeset by RefineCatch Limited, Bungay, Suffolk

This book is sold subject to the condition that it shall not, by way of trade or otherwise, be lent, resold, hired out, or otherwise circulated without the publisher's prior consent in any form of binding or cover other than that in which it is published and without a similar condition including this condition being imposed on the subsequent purchaser.

A C.I.P. listing for this book is available on request.

CHAPTER 1

James is having lunch with his mistress, Geraldine, at his club in Soho. Usually, on a Wednesday lunchtime, he'd be having it off with her in her Islington flat but today they've both told the other that their schedules are tight at the moment and that a quick lunch in town is all either of them can really manage.

James watches her arrive with Beckett, that dysfunctional dog of hers. He sees her embark on the obligatory argument with the restaurant manager, the same one she has with every maître d' in London, the one where she explains that the dog goes everywhere with her and yes, she knows about health and safety but her dog is, she can assure them, cleaner than most of his customers. She thinks that she gets her way because of her persuasive argument; the fact is, of course, that they make an exception because of who she is dining with – him: James Marlborough; someone who is not only the most accomplished actor of his generation but also too much of a gentleman ever to point this out to her.

It occurs to him that her repulsive dog is something else he will not miss when he tells her their relationship is over.

Which is what he is about to do.

Yes. This is going to be hard for her but it has to be done. When they started their affair she was directing some of the best theatre around and she was absolutely the right person for an actor of his standing to be connected with. Then she made the crazy move from theatre to TV and was really no longer any use to him at all. He had planned to end it then, four months ago, when she made her grand announcement about her career change. But it seemed churlish to stop things while he was still enjoying sex with her as much as he did so he persisted with the relationship against his better judgement, romantic fool that he is.

The thing about Geraldine is that she likes sex like a man does – aggressive, rough, obvious. So bloody refreshing after all these women who want endless cajoling and coaxing before they'll take their knickers off. What's more, Geraldine likes to have Shakespeare recited to her while she's being penetrated. It's the iambic pentameter, apparently, which helps her climax. And James has rather enjoyed that, having a woman so excited by his oration that it brought her to orgasm. But now it really is time to make a break and start shagging his leading lady in Lear. Historically he has always had sexual relations with his leading ladies in his plays, he has always found that the production goes ahead much more smoothly when he does – which is only human nature when you think about it.

He hopes that Geraldine won't make a fuss.

He watches her making her way over to the table.

As always he is somewhat overwhelmed by her, by his powerful sexual craving for her tinged with the slight, very subtle yet indisputable sense of physical revulsion she produces in him. He has never been able to work out whether the craving is in spite of the revulsion or because of it but another positive aspect of ending it with her will be that this dilemma will no longer be a problem any more. She is not, conventionally speaking, attractive; he has always known that. Everything about Geraldine is long and straight – her jet black hair, her nose, her fingers. She looks like a Modigliani in a trouser suit. Her lips are thin and tight. Her chest is flat. Her skin is so pale it is vaguely blue. Her green eyes are narrow and tilt up sardonically at the end. The next one he has lined up, the actress playing Cordelia, is younger than Geraldine, with better tits and fuller lips. The prospect of that gives him courage, as does another large swig of the rather marvellous Zinfandel he has ordered. He had wanted to do all this by text, but some sixth sense told him Geraldine was a woman better dumped in person. So here he is, honourable to the bloody end.

He really, really hopes that Geraldine won't make a fuss. She is a woman addicted to melodrama at the best of times and he rather fears that for her this will be one of the worst, poor girl.

She arrives at the table, avec dog, exuberant, triumphant, her long arms flapping with appeased indignation. 'So much fuss about one small canine,' she drones. She spreads open her handbag which converts semi-automatically into a portable dog bed and puts her animal in it. 'Go sleepies,' she tells the dog and he immediately does. Then she scans the restaurant for anyone she recognises who might be worth acknowledging with a cry, a wave, a blown kiss or even, if they are truly significant, a quick trip over to their table. Seeing no one who merits any of these accolades she lavishly adjusts her hair, scarves, jewellery so that everyone can see it is her, Geraldine Fortescue, who is amongst them, and when she perceives this fact to have been suitably recognised she concludes that stage of the performance and finally sits down.

She looks at James.

She has come to lunch today to tell him it's over between them. It's lasted longer than most of her affairs and has been pleasant but she needs to move on. For a while she thought it might be a good idea that she retained a key contact in theatre while she waited to see whether she could successfully transfer her skills from theatre to TV but as her new career seems to be working out so wonderfully well his part in it now appears redundant. She'd be much better off switching her affections to a producer or someone in charge of media spend. And it's not just the professional angle that's the problem, Geraldine's not that shallow. It's the sexual thing too. His demands are getting more and more peculiar. She is tired of having to adjust Beckett's collar to fit James neck so that he can wear it to strut round her apartment woofing and demanding that she throw Beckett's toys for him so he can romp over to them and fetch them back to her. All the "good boy deserves a treat" and "bad boy deserves punishment" stuff seemed such a laugh at first but now it's starting to grate and most of the time when she's with him she wishes he would just go sleepies too. It's true, she concedes to herself, that she will miss the Shakespeare passages in bed but if she gets it together with that TV mogul she's got in mind the thought of increasing her ratings will probably bring her to orgasm just as quickly.

'How are rehearsals going?' she begins politely.

Of course, James thinks. We should make small talk first. Get the food ordered, be civilised about it all. He pours her a glass of wine.

'Very well,' he replies. 'Yes, superbly well in fact' he adds with a tone to suggest that, given his involvement, any alternative is hardly feasible. 'And how is work with you?' he asks Geraldine back because he knows women expect that sort of thing.

'Fabulous!' Geraldine enthuses.

'This is the mother and famous offspring thing?' James enquires idly.

'James, you know it is,' Geraldine retorts irritably. 'It's "I Gave Birth To A Celebrity", the project I've been working on for months now. I'm the producer and the presenter – everything is in my control. It will be superb television and costs peanuts to make. We're paying the celebrities nothing but even so they're falling over themselves to take part.'

'So who's the first celebrity you've got?'

'Aha!' Geraldine teases. 'Wouldn't you like to know!'

No, actually, I don't give a fuck, James thinks.

Geraldine snorts. 'You'll have to wait and see. The surprise is everything, James! The day after tomorrow I'm going off to film the interview with the mother on her own at her house. I'll just drop a few hints, nothing that will ever stand up in court, that her beloved celebrity child has been, well, less than complimentary about her parenting skills. Then bam – it'll all come out, all the resentment, jealousy, frustration will all pour forth like sewage from a drain. The show itself will go out live that same evening, with the mother and daughter on stage in front of an audience. We'll have a bit of small talk then we'll play the film back to them on a huge screen at the back of the stage. It's a guaranteed formula for televisual trauma!' Geraldine concludes with a flourish.

James looks unsure. 'Oh. Is that wise?'

'It's not about wisdom, James, it's about viewing figures. And really I'm doing these mothers and their successful children a favour, exposing some profound psychological truths to them about how they really feel about each other. Success is only ever achieved by people who have suffered difficult childhoods. When, if, they survive my programme they can all go off and have some analysis and really discover themselves. I tell you, I'm doing them a favour.'

'Geraldine darling, you got a first in English from Cambridge, you are the best theatre director there is, I still for the life of me can't understand why the hell you've decided to pack it all in to make bloody television.'

Geraldine smiles and rubs the fingers of one hand together to indicate recompense.

'Yes, OK, but really – why that kind of television? Popular dross!'

Geraldine finds James so tedious when he gets on his high horse like this. He's a bloody thespian snob. It's very boring. 'Really darling, you must understand – theatre has had its day. Television is now the only medium worth bothering with. With the programmes I make I will become a twenty-first century chronicler of contemporary culture, the Chaucer of my age! I will tell the stories about people the way they really live and think, just as he did!'

'Bollocks,' says James.

Geraldine is shocked. He usually loves her hyperbole. He has never spoken to her like this before. She picks up an olive and sucks on it, seeking out the pimiento pepper with her tongue. Normally this would drive him wild with desire. Now he looks merely bored with the whole thing. She winds her shiny pink tongue round the olive and pulls on the scarlet stuffing to suck it slowly out. Then she puts her tongue slowly in and out of the hole left in the olive and stares hard at him to make sure he gets the message. He plays absent-mindedly with his cutlery.

What is wrong with him?

Geraldine cannot bear James' indifference. She may be about to chuck him but that does not give him the right to treat her with such disinterest. She takes her stockinged foot out of her shoe and starts to massage his genitalia with it under the table. The waitress brings them the menu and hovers. Geraldine looks at James and says to the waitress, 'The thing is, I can't decide whether I'd rather have something hard or something soft in my mouth.'

'Oh?' says the girl, who is used to erratic behaviours – this is a private club for actors after all.

'Yes. I'm wondering, you see, I'm wondering whether I'd rather suck on something round and fleshy – like a ripe fig or a lightly grilled scallop,' Geraldine muses while sketching the outline of James' scrotum with her big toe. 'Or whether I wouldn't prefer something more robust with more body to it, like a firm, bulbous fennel or the rounded contour of a lovely ripe Conference pear,' she deliberates as her toe moves up and down and round and round.

James, much to his annoyance, feels his dick start to respond to her attentions under the table. His balls jump and expand, swelling tight with desire. Dammit. He can hardly dump the woman while he's got a hard-on for her. As Geraldine feels him inflate and stiffen she smiles with relief, her thin, taut lips stretching winsomely across her face like a crack in a dish. For one horrible moment she thought she no longer had control over her redundant lover.

'Our specials today are leek and stilton soup and venison stew,' sighs the girl, bored with constantly having to provide a one-woman audience for the impromptu recitals of the customers she serves who have taken too seriously the diktat that all the world's a stage. She's had an offer of a job in her local dry cleaners and while Balham isn't Soho, it might be preferable to putting up with this kind of bullshit all the time. 'I'll come back when you're ready,' she says.

James, tense with inappropriate desire, is indignant at this attitude. 'Hang on, hang on there!' he barks. 'We're not ready for you to go!' If he can't have Geraldine now he needs to take his frustration out on someone, for Christ's sake.

'Do you know what you want then?' the girl asks.

'No, but it's not going to kill you to wait until we do, is it?'

'So – you want me to just stand here and watch and wait for you to make up your minds?'

'Do you know who I am?' James asks simply.

The waitress looks at him like she gives a shit and goes to serve the next table.

James immediately feels like a fool. Geraldine, now confident that she has still got him where she wants him, removes her foot and offers him a sour look which, on her face, is easily achieved.

'Really, James,' she admonishes, 'that was rather pompous, don't you think?'

She seems so cocky, so detached, so unlike her normal self where she is usually fawning all over him.

Jesus – what if she is about to chuck him? Yes, it's unthinkable, he knows, but women are capable of behaving most irrationally when least expected. He'd better make his move quickly, he doesn't want her getting her oar in first.

Just then Geraldine sees coming into the restaurant one of the powerful TV executives she has been considering for James' replacement. She can see he's seen her. Perfect. Perfect! She leans over intimately towards James. 'Anyway, enough about work. Let's talk about sex. I'm missing you, bad boy,' she announces with a voice loud enough to reach the tables at the back. 'You big, big, big, bad boy. When are we going to have a lovely big shag again?'

James falls back in his chair with relief. Thank God; she is still as devoted as ever; he must have just been imagining things. His erection kicks in, harder than before. His mouth grows dry with lust. 'Darling, really, some discretion, everyone will hear!' he pleads delightedly. Perhaps he should fit in one last bonk with her before he ends it.

The TV executive man waves and smiles enthusiastically in Geraldine's direction and gestures to his mobile phone to show he'll be calling her before walking away with his guests down towards a private dining area in the club. Geraldine is thrilled.

'What did you say?' she asks, nonchalantly turning her attention back towards James.

'I said, Geraldine, you must show some discretion here – people know me.'

'Oh, for God's sake,' says Geraldine irritably, 'don't be such a bore. Everyone here is married to someone else, you can't really imagine that anyone gives a toss what you're up to.'

Once again James feels assuaged by doubt. She looks bored silly by him. This is no good. He can't afford to take the risk of waiting to see if she is going to end it or not – he has to make his move. He can use what she's just said as his cue. James likes to work on cues. Now she's introduced the subject of marriage he can blame having to leave her on Serena, that'll make everything much easier.

'Yes, well, to be honest, I'm glad you brought it up.'

'For Christ's sake, James, I'm about to have lunch, can we talk about the state of your penis some other time?'

'No, no, I don't mean that. I mean, I'm glad you brought up the marriage thing. Because the point is Geraldine, I've been thinking and, well, you know, Serena dotes on me and if she were to find out about us, well, it would simply devastate her.'

'Can a woman with so little brain be capable of devastation? The occasional small, sporadic twitch of cognitive function perhaps – but devastation?' Geraldine asks pleasantly.

'Geraldine, I think we should end things now. I feel such . . . guilt. I must go back to my marriage and put things right between Serena and me.'

'Are you being serious?'

'Oh yes, totally,' says James offering her a really serious expression to prove it.

'Who the hell do you think you are, giving me the married man's speech about guilt and remorse? You bastard! You've been shagging me since last Christmas and now you want to end it just like that? Who do you think I am? I'm not some tawdry make-up girl you can simply take up with, screw and then abandon at will. Things with me aren't as easy as that!' she hollers.

'Yes, I'm aware of that,' says James mournfully. How tiresome this leaving them bit always is. It's a wonder it didn't put him off starting a new affair each time, knowing there was always this nonsense to contend with at the end of it.

'You might not like it but you have always known I'm married, that I have a commitment to my wife, that I have to consider her feelings above everything, even my own! You can understand that, can't you? Be reasonable, please,' James whines.

'Reasonable? You were hardly calling for reason the last time we were together when you followed me naked round my flat on all fours, barking and wanting me to throw Beckett's chews for you. How reasonable was that?' Geraldine retorts with fury.

Jesus, why did he ever start anything with this woman? She may be successful but she's a pain in the arse. He should have stuck with make-up girls and script editors, the young, grateful ones who were always so much easier.

'Geraldine, you know sex between us has been amazing,

but it was always just going to be a bit of fun wasn't it? It was never going to last, we both knew that.'

'I never knew that, when did you tell me that?'

'Well, it was . . .' James sweats, his eyes full of supplication, 'it was obvious.'

'No, James, that's not good enough,' Geraldine commands. 'It was never obvious to me. And, in fact, now that we're finally discussing it, I have decided that I want you to leave Serena, James. I want you to leave her for me.'

Here we go, thinks James. The time-honoured why-can't-you-leave-your-wife-for-me routine; they all get there sooner or later. 'Look, don't start all that,' he complains. 'You know why I can't leave Serena. It's just not going to happen. It would break her heart and, even more importantly, it would ruin my career. She's the most famous TV actress in the country and when people know I'm married to her, well, it's just bums on seats, isn't it?'

'Don't be ridiculous, you've won six Oliviers and two Tonys. You don't need to rely on that bit of fluff to feel confident about your success.'

'You say that – but look at you! You've decamped, you know the power of television better than anyone.'

'What about sex? You told me that you find the very sight of her so off-putting you can't face doing it with her any more.'

Dammit, dammit. This is true. In a mistaken moment of tenderness James had confessed that he's so sick of his silly wife that he finds the prospect of having sex with her quite nauseating. He sees her vacuous face, hears her sharp, squeaky voice and instantaneously his manhood nose-dives. Whereas with Geraldine it's all he can do to stop the thing exploding. What can he do? He doesn't love his wife and he doesn't love his mistress either but she's the only one his willy appears to work with.

'Is that true? Is it true you no longer have sex with her?'

'Yes, yes, it is,' James gasps.

'You know if I were to find out you were lying to me my fury would know no bounds.'

'Yes, Geraldine, I do know that,' James whimpers.

'So?' says Geraldine, licking her lower lip. 'Are you going to leave her or not?'

She sees James prevaricating.

Jesus, he really is thinking about it!

She decides to see how far she can push it. Taking people to the very limits of their endurance is one of Geraldine's favourite sports.

'James, you must leave her. Otherwise I will have to tell her about us.'

Why do all ex-girlfriends make the same threats? They use the same words, the same tone, they even the same facial expressions. There's no originality, no bloody variety, just the same script repeated over and over. The sense of déjà vu is so powerful for poor James that he feels almost overwhelmed by it.

'Oh please, Geraldine, don't do anything stupid, don't tell her.' He knows his lines. He knows this is the stage where you have to beg to placate them. 'My career would fall to pieces if she left me!'

'Do you think she'll enjoy hearing how her husband likes to wear a collar and lead and sit on my lap and eat dog biscuits while I rub his tummy?' Geraldine enquires loudly.

'You've got no proof!' he retaliates weakly.

'No proof? Seize the day, my darling, seize the day,' she murmurs victoriously as her big toe returns to his crotch to make contact with the words 'CARPE DIEM' which James had tattooed the length of his member in a moment of inebriated insanity in his youth.

She watches James' face crinkle purple with fear. He opens his mouth to speak but nothing comes out. 'So now are you still so sure that "it's just not going to happen"? Are you?'

'What I meant was,' James stammers, his mouth now dry

with something other than desire, something more like abject terror, 'all I meant by that was it's not going to happen now, right now, but of course, in the future, well, the future is different isn't it? We never know what might happen then.'

'And by future we mean what? Next week, next month, next year, next incarnation perhaps?' Her big toe is kneading its way ever deeper between his legs. The erection bounces back. He gasps with pleasure and pain. His temples start thudding with rage while his groin continues to pulsate with desire. How can he feel both fury and longing simultaneously for the same woman?

'All right, all right, I'll tell her – soon.'

'Soon?' Geraldine enquires, working ever further into the scrotal tissue.

'OK, now!!'

'You swear?'

'I swear. I'll tell her all about us and sort everything out,' he stutters. 'Only please, don't say anything to Serena. And please, please, stop doing what you're doing down there, yes, that, with your foot. I can't hold back much longer if you don't stop.'

Geraldine laughs. What fun this is.

'I'll only stop if you do some lines with me,' Geraldine demands triumphantly.

'Are you crazy?' James begs. 'In a restaurant? Now? In a public place? Don't be ridiculous! You know what that'll do to you!'

'Do lines or I'll tell wifey where I keep your chews and squeaky toys in that box in my study!' Geraldine cries.

'Oh for God's sake, all right, all right but be discreet, please.'

'Of course, darling,' Geraldine grins.

So James leans across the table to her and, sottovoce, begins:

'To 't, luxury, pell-mell! for I lack soldiers.

Behold yond simpering dame, Whose face between her forks presages snow;

That mines virtue, and does shake the head
To hear of pleasure's name;'

The moment he begins to speak it is like the turning on of a tap and Geraldine feels herself getting damp with desire for him.

James sees the reaction in her face and stops. 'Go on!' she hisses, 'Go on!'

Nervously he whispers:
'The fitchew, nor the soiled horse, goes to 't
With a more riotous appetite . . .'

Geraldine shuts her eyes in ecstasy.

What a pity. She is going to miss all this when she dumps him. Which she will do, of course, just as soon as he ends his marriage for her. She doesn't want him. She has no desire whatsoever to be with him. She just wants him to leave his wife before she lets him know that. It'll teach him not to mess with women of her calibre (not that there are any others). It'll pay him back for even thinking of dumping her. It'll show the bastard who he's dealing with.

James continues with his recital. God. He may be a bastard but he can deliver a line. She feels her blood begin to ripple and bubble in her veins. His timbre seeps into her stomach and up between her legs where it quakes and thunders. She feels her lips part and moisten with awe. Ah! The power of the delivery; the flawlessness of the tone! Her skin pricks and blisters with wonder at the words as they filter through her consciousness into her soul. She slips her hand down between her legs and begins rhythmically with her fingers to honour the splendour of the language.

At this point the waitress remembers them and starts walking back towards the table to take their order. She can see the man leaning across burbling some kind of smut to the woman who is quite clearly bringing herself off with her hand under the table while she listens. The waitress puts down her pad, takes off her apron and leaves. A life of percholorethylene fumes will be bliss compared to this.

CHAPTER 2

'Oh, Barry, Barry – if only you weren't my husband's brother's son!' cries Sue.

'But it doesn't matter, I tell you! I'm 22, a grown man, I can make my own choices,' cries Barry back. 'More than that, Sue, we are in love! That's got to be more important than anything!'

'Is it? I wish it was. I really do. I really, really do. But if my husband, Gary, or his brother who is your dad and called Tony were to find out – we'd both be done for!'

'I don't care about my dad or his brother who is my uncle Gary and your husband! All I care about is you, Sue. I want to kiss you. I want to take you in my arms and kiss you long and hard and then make love to you!'

'But what about the fact that you work for your dad, my husband Gary's brother, Tony? You help him in his business selling cars and he's been doing some dodgy deals and the people he owes money to are on their way over there now and only you know about it and if you're not there in half an hour they're going to beat him up and leave him for dead? And what about your uncle Gary, my husband, who is your father Tony's brother – he lent you that money so you could pay off your gambling debts – how can you do this to him?! And your fiancée, Diane, my best friend's bridesmaid, pregnant with twins after six years IVF, what about her?'

'I don't care, Sue! You are the only woman for me! My love for you is stronger than anything! Let me kiss you, Sue. I have to kiss you! I have to have you now!'

'Oh, Barry, I should stay away but I can't. Your dark, strong, good looks are intoxicating me, your young, firm, muscular body is enticing me ever closer to you, you're luring me in, you're captivating me, you're – sweating.'

'What?'

'You're sweating! He's sweating! Again! I told you last time, I won't do a sweaty close-up, I won't!'

Serena throws down her script, folds her arms and sticks out her lower lip.

'All right, Serena, darling, don't panic,' Terry, the director cuts in, panicking, recognising the signs of imminent strop. 'We'll get make-up to tidy him up, angel.'

'OK, I agree, there is a bit of perspiration on my brow,' Brian complains as a girl with a large brush caked in orange descends upon him, 'but it's only what you'd expect, isn't it? This is a passionate love scene!'

Serena rolls her eyes and pouts and sighs. She's being as patient as she can with this bloke but there are limits. As if it isn't hard enough to be working with a man called Brian. Does he really expect her, Serena Dawlish, to snog him when he's dripping?

'Let me tell you something, Bry-anne,' she begins, 'a professional actor does not sweat.'

'What?'

'No. He doesn't. He controls his sweat. Do you see me sweating? No. That's because I'm a professional, I know what I'm doing and I –'

Terry swerves across and pulls her firmly away by the elbow. 'Come on, Serena, baby,' he urges into her dainty pink ear. 'Don't give him such a hard time. It's difficult for the boy, he's working with you, the famous Serena Dawlish. You're looking fucking gorgeous, darling, you can hardly blame the guy for breaking out in a sweat. He probably has your poster on his bedroom wall and goes to sleep every night wanking off looking at it,' Terry jokes, to lighten things a bit.

Serena sighs again. 'I suppose you're right, Terry. But you know what I'm like – I give it my all and I want it right first time.'

'I know, I know. You're a star, we all know that. So are you OK now, babe? Can we get going again?'

Serena pouts and tuts and considers. 'Oh, OK,' she groans. She rearranges her extensions so they fall, softly, naturally, over her shoulders, and adjusts the silicon in her chest which always seems to go funny when she gets upset.

Brian resurfaces from the attentions of the make-up girl. He's got an outsize satsuma on his neck. He's not pleased. He doesn't want to be caked in dayglo foundation but worse than the embarrassment is the pain in his heart. Because Brian is sweating because he's not acting. Brian is sweating because he really is in real love with the woman in his arms.

'OK,' Terry yells, 'we'll take it from, "I don't care, Sue!"'

Brian is feeling giddy with passion, his heart is thudding so hard it's all he can do to breathe, much less speak his lines. Can't she see that? He forces himself on.

'I don't care, Sue!' he croaks. 'You are the only woman for me! My love for you is stronger than anything! Let me kiss you, Sue. I have to kiss you! I have to have you now!'

'Oh, Barry, I should stay away but I can't, your dark, strong, good looks are intoxicating me, your young, firm, muscular body is enticing me ever closer to you, you're luring me in – have you gargled?'

'What?'

'Will you stop saying "what", OK? You're doing my head in! Terry, he's doing my head in!'

'But "have you gargled?" isn't in the script!' Brian complains.

'Have you at least sucked on a mint? We're about to do the big kiss, it's a matter of courtesy, not to say professional consideration, you know.'

'Are you saying my breath smells?' Brian barks at her in a whisper.

'I'm saying that, as an actress, there are limits to what I can reasonably be expected to do on set,' she replies.

Terry wants to weep. 'Serena, I'm begging you, can we just get through this? It's the big kiss coming up, you know how important that scene is.'

'OK, OK,' says Serena, holding her hands up. 'But I'll be talking to my manager about this and he is not going to be happy.'

She picks up her script again. 'The thing is,' Serena wails elegantly, 'ever since I lost the baby and my dad got run over and my business selling lingerie folded I've felt so alone, so alone and now, now it's hard for me to believe that anyone could ever want me – as a woman.' She looks up at Brian, as best as she can through the fur of false eyelashes glued to her lids. Brian looks back at her, at those large, juicy, red lips; at her long, auburn, waist-length, tousled, shiny hair as it tumbles down over the enormous breasts billowing under his face.

He must remember to act.

'I want you so much, Sue.'

'I don't believe you. I'm a nothing. I'm worthless. All my life I've been treated so bad – rejected, abandoned, neglected, ignored. How, how could anyone want me?' she whispers and starts gently to sob small, pretty sobs.

At this point filming has to stop again as a couple of the sound and cameramen have started to laugh. When they have suitably composed themselves, Serena says, 'What is it you want from me, Barry?'

'I've told you. I want you to kiss me, that's all.'

'A simple kiss?'

'Yes.'

He plays lovingly with her curls. Serena feels herself about to lose it again. If he yanks any harder at that lock of hair it's going to come off in his hands, the weave can only take so much messing about with. He traces a finger lightly over her lips – which is a waste of his time because since the last dose of collagen Serena can't feel anything there anyway.

'Those lips, those warm, sensual lips, I cannot resist them,' he murmurs and starts lurching further towards her.

Serena can tell, even before his moist, eager mouth makes contact with hers, that he has in fact, just as she suspected, not gargled even though her contract states perfectly clearly that she only does open-mouth kissing with actors who have rinsed their mouths thoroughly beforehand with a suitable anti-bacterial mouthwash of a recognised brand.

His lips meet hers. They start to kiss.

★

Serena tries to analyse forensically what it is that Brian might have eaten which has given his mouth this peculiar taste it's got and eventually decides that it's not a question of food, just general oral malfunction. It isn't pleasant but when you're a professional this is what you do, you get on with it. At least she, Serena, is paid to put up with it. But what she wonders is why don't the girlfriends of these men who kiss them out of choice, why don't they tell them how slimy the inside of their mouths are? And why don't these men notice it themselves, that every time they open their gobs a strange odour pervades the atmosphere? These are the things Serena thinks about as she rolls around on sofas, car seats, beds, any padded surface really because her contract states no physical discomfort, snogging the man she shouldn't be doing it with while she's waiting for the man she should be doing it with to turn up and discover her doing it.

Meanwhile the camera swoops in on their locked jaws. Serena makes some sexual ecstasy noise in the back of her throat. She's famous for, well, everything really, but especially for her kissing noise. It's a noise that's hard to describe, sort of a bit like the noise you make when you've been desperate for a wee and finally make it, that sort of 'aaaah' of relief but all done in the throat of course, the mouth being otherwise engaged.

Because, let's face it, noise is important. People think telly is all about what people look like – that's where they're wrong. Of course, yes, looks do matter, and the fact that Serena is The Most Attractive Woman In A Soap doesn't do any harm. By the way, that's not just her saying it, it's the readers of 'Turn Me On' magazine, the widest read TV listings publication in the country, who have voted her there for three years running, so it's scientifically proven, so to speak. But Serena's point is this: have you ever tried watching TV with the sound down? And how does it look? Stupid, that's how. Because the sound is what counts, and that's not just the words people say but the actual sounds they make. Serena understands this. She has worked hard on her noises; that's just one of the reasons why she's at the top of her game and the other girls are not. You could say, and Serena does, that she's perfected the art of noise – sexual noise. It is, in fact, very difficult to make good sexual noise. Most people aren't aware of this. They just don't give it much thought. They see Serena in action and think – sit on a sofa and snog a bloke – anyone can do that. But have they ever seen themselves doing it? Heard themselves doing it? Of course they haven't. And it wouldn't be a pretty sight or sound if they did. The truth of the matter is there's an art to putting your tongue down the back of a bloke's throat and making it look nice and, most of all, making it sound nice. All the other girls in the soaps either whimper like they're about to pass out or do this weird grunting thing like they're about to lay an egg. Frankly it's embarrassing.

But because Serena is a professional actress (yes, actress: Serena is proud of her sex and doesn't buy into all that call-me-an-actor crap) she has practised noise in her bedroom mirror for hour after hour and even when in the act with her husband. He didn't need to know that many, OK all, of the gurgles of pleasure she used to make (used to because she doesn't make them any more now she's perfected them) were part of her professional endeavours to have the best repertoire of sexual noises of any actress in any soap. And it's all paid off handsomely because now she hears the director saying stuff to the other girls like, 'Can you make it sound like you're enjoying it a little more, please, Jasmine,?' or, 'Couldn't you give it a bit more oomph when he's on top of you, Lynsey?' Whereas when she's on set Terry doesn't say a word and everyone's electrified by her explosions of passion. The fact is that Serena brings a certain dedication to her profession which the other soap actresses just aren't capable of. She's raised the industry standard, that's what she's done and she knows it and she's proud of it, proud of her contribution to television.

*

At this point it says in the script that Barry should break away from the kiss, look at Sue and cry 'My God, you're lovely!' then re-attach himself to her with even more vigour. That's the bit where she can come up for a bit of air. Of course she can breathe while kissing but it's not exactly good quality oxygen down there at the coal face of Brian's ungargled tonsils. A break gives her a chance to really fill her lungs before she gets stuck back into another bout. It's a bit like being a professional flautist in a classical orchestra, she always thinks. They have to take a deep breath when they can, before they really go for it on those long bits. There's quite a bit in common, actually, when you think about it, between an actress in a soap and a classically trained musician – control, commitment, determination, all sorts of stuff.

But Barry's not doing it. He's not breaking away.

Terry must have realised that Barry should've done it by now, just to give her a bit of a breather, but he's not stopping the scene, the bastard, because he knows it's going really well, the viewers love a good necking, and he's letting it drag on. It's moments like this – he knows it, she knows it – which make the difference in the ratings, therefore the amount they can charge in the ads, therefore Terry's fee. It annoys Serena to know that it's her oral performance which is lining Terry's pocket. He's exploiting her, that's what he's doing, and yes, the more tea bags and mortgages the show sells the more she earns too but that's not the point, is it?, because it's her coping with Brian's oral hygiene issues right now, isn't it?, not him, not Terry.

Anyway, whatever, Serena tells herself. She has to calm down and get on with the job. She opens her mouth a bit wider and pushes forward the muscles in her lips, what little she can still feel well enough to control behind the rolls of rubber inside them. That way they jut out more on the man's face – that always goes down well. And she makes more noise.

*

Before she knows it, her mind is wandering again. She should really just concentrate on the kiss and not let her thoughts keep going off at a tangent, but the thing is, you see, Serena is a thinking woman, what can she do about that?, she's always had a very active brain. Not at school, no, not at Gerrards Cross County Grammar, but that was their problem, they just didn't understand her there. They didn't realise what they were dealing with and how much acting meant to her, even then. OK, so she was crap at exams but hello, who was always the star at the end of term productions? Who had the dads coming back to see the school play every night it was on to watch her act her heart out in her very short skirts? And still the teachers whinged and complained, bunch of old dykes the lot of them, and told her mum and dad at parents evenings that she just didn't have what it takes to do GCSEs and it was like, GCSEs? Who wants to do bloody GCSEs anyway! Judge me on my art!

After she finished school, when she was asked to leave but was going to leave anyway actually, Serena worked for years as a waitress in Gerrards Cross and her talent lay dormant. In fact, it might never have been discovered had not one day someone given her a piece of good advice: they said if you want to be an actress you need to hang around where other actors are and she thought about it and she thought – acting – Shakespeare – Stratford. So she went and got herself a job as a barmaid in the pub in Stratford where all the actors went after the play and it worked, it really worked! Some guy chatted her up; it turned out he was the most famous of the lot of them, not that she would know, Shakespeare not really being her thing. So guess what – she only went and ended up marrying him! And then someone he knew got her introduced to someone who was looking for a woman to play a walk-on part in 'Coombe Ridge Crescent,' the most popular soap in Britain. She turned that part into the starring role – and that was how TV history was made.

*

Meanwhile Brian's little tongue is still wriggling about in her mouth like an overactive earthworm. Someone told her recently – she can't remember who – that there's a direct link between the size of a man's tongue and his willy. Which stands to reason when you think about it. This makes Serena wonder. This Brian looks like a well-built chap but his tongue is a funny thin little thing, in which case . . .

Anyway the point is this – whatever the size of it, he should be keeping his tongue still. The contract says open mouth but no internal movement. Really she should stop the scene, stop it now, but this is the last one of the day and she's desperate to get out and round to that boutique which has just had a delivery of the new donkey skin handbag which they're holding for her just because she's her and which she wants to be seen with before anyone else is seen with it. So she just keeps going like the bloody trouper she is. She gives up all hope of Barry stopping things of his own accord, that's just not going to happen, she can tell that much. She's simply going to have to hang on in there now until the bit in the script where her husband, Gary, stumbles into the house when he comes back unexpectedly in the middle of the day to pick up the credit card he had forgotten which he was going to use to go to the jewellers and buy her a 25 carat diamond ring to celebrate their first year's wedding anniversary – Sue's longest relationship yet.

Come on, Gary, come on, Serena thinks, come and rescue me before my mouth furs up like the inside of a kettle.

*

Barry's still hard at it kissing her; time is still passing, slowly; Serena is getting really bored now. She thinks more about the handbag, what colour she should do her nails next, whether that navy blue eyeliner really goes with her green eye shadow and whether she's going to be on the cover of that week's issue of 'The Soap Box' or not. But then she stops herself. She shouldn't allow herself to daydream like this. She's a pro, she has to keep herself in role, really focus on the scene in hand. At this point, talking of hands, she notices that somewhere along the line, Brian's hand has moved down from her shoulder where he has manfully grabbed her, as indicated in the script, to her chest area, as not indicated in the script. Surely Terry will see this and put a stop to things? Surely? Because breast fondling is so not in her contract and if Brian doesn't get his grubby paw back on her shoulder sharpish she'll stop things her bloody self and she'll sue. There was that other guy last year who'd tried it on, same thing exactly, except no, maybe she was on top of him that time, yes, she was on top of him, and his hands started wandering and she stopped things then and complained. The actor said it wasn't his fault, her tits were so big there was nowhere else for his hands to go, everywhere he tried to put them her chest was there and she thought, fair enough, he's got a point, because Serena is all woman, inside and out, she is just so well-endowed and that's just nature really, isn't it?, nothing you can do about that.

Anyway, to keep things on an even course Serena shifts and twists and writhes about a bit, just to let Brian know, subtly, that he's on a hiding to nothing but of course when you've got a body like hers any sort of movement it makes is so provocative, so tantalising, she just can't help it, it just can't help it, that of course it only gets poor Brian going all the more and now he's the one making the noises. Rather strange noises, actually. Sort of rasping, gasping noises like he's about to . . . well, take things that one step too far. For a soap, anyway.

Serena's concerned for him. He hasn't been in the cast for long, he just hasn't got the experience. She'd better check how far things have gone. He might be in a really bad way and need help. With her right hand, the one that's tucked down well away from the cameras, she reaches out, carefully, sensitively, just to see if, well, to see if it's all getting too much for him, if he's letting himself get carried away. Because it does happen, of course it does, and these poor actors, who can blame them, they're only men after all, aren't they? There they are, surrounded by the crew, they arrive on set all prepared to do their bit as best they can and before they know it they're in the arms of Serena Dawlish, this country's top soap actress, and suddenly they are out of their depth, just flailing around, drowning with desire and it's up to her to find a way to rescue them before they make a complete prat of themselves in front of everyone. With the sort of expertly dextrous homing action that only comes with years of experience, Serena surreptitiously locates his manhood – purely for professional purposes, of course. Oh my God. Oh my God. It's as she suspected. He's past the point of no return. He's crossed the line from acting to actuality. Why can these men never stick to what's printed on the sheet they're given? His trousers are hot to the touch, faintly damp and clearly ready to burst with the swelling, pulsating thing inside them. She is there for him, she really is. All she wants to do is help a fellow colleague in distress, so gently but firmly, well out of sight of camera, she starts to stroke it with the palm of her hand, to soothe it, calm it, get it to relax before it does something stupid.

Brian's noises behind the kiss, meanwhile, grow more

urgent and peculiar, as if he is being strangled, yes, that's the closest description she can think of. Why doesn't he let her help him? With her firm, sure hand she palpates harder and harder until she's practically squeezing his crotch into a state of greater repose but, silly boy, the more she rubs the stiffer he grows and the more desperate the noises coming up from his throat and it seems as if his trousers are about to explode when suddenly, after what seems like a century, in crashes Gary, her husband. About bloody time. Brian quickly pulls his mouth away from hers. Unfortunately their lips, after being sealed together for so long, have created a sort of suctioned vacuum and when they finally come apart there is an unpleasant sort of plopping sound. Never mind, they can always edit that one out and, to be honest, after the sort of stifled pantings Brian's been making up till now one more strange noise isn't going to make that much difference, is it?

So right on cue Gary finds them together and cries, 'Sue! You bitch!', and she gives him a look which combines terror, pride and defiance – it's one of the best looks from her selection – and Barry runs stumbling from the room and Serena gasps, 'Gary – it's you who I really love!' and on this triumphant note Terry brings down the clapboard and calls it a day.

*

Terry is well pleased with the scene. He comes up and starts cooing and clucking over Serena, telling her she just keeps getting better with every episode, wondering where all her talent comes from, blah blah blah. Tell her something she doesn't know. She considers having a go at him about allowing Brian to skip the pulling away bit and letting the kiss go on for at least three minutes longer than it should have done but then thinks, what's the point, Brian's only flesh and blood, she can hardly blame him for trying and anyway, she wants to get out and get that handbag. So she goes back to her dressing room and starts to get changed but, well, it's strange, because she is in a hurry to leave but the thing is that kiss, it's sort of got her going. It has. Because she's a very sensual woman, Serena is, very tactile. Her psychic told her she has gypsy blood in her from several generations back and she can really believe it, she can really feel a strong, earthy drive in her you wouldn't normally associate with a girl from Gerrards Cross. So once she is undressed she pops on a flimsy silk robe and gets one of the girls from production to nip across the corridor to Brian's dressing room to tell him Serena wants a word.

Within moments Brian appears at the door. 'You OK, love?' she says, letting the robe fall casually open, ushering him in.

Brian looks at her – a look of shock, terror and desire. That's a good combo look, Serena thinks to herself. I should remember that one.

'What? Am I OK? Of course I'm not bloody OK!' he cries. 'You know what happened in there. That kiss – we weren't acting! Neither of us! That was real, Serena!'

Oh dear, here we go again, Serena sighs. Just as she thought. They just can't handle it.

'I'm in love with you! Really in love! You must realise that! Every time I see you I get this hot, burning sensation between my legs.'

Serena grimaces. 'Do you think it might be thrush?'

'I love you! Why won't you believe me?' he cries.

'Look, Barry, love –'

'It's Brian!'

'Yes, of course, sorry – Brian. Look, what can I say. Don't kid yourself, sweetheart. You have to understand the divide between reality and fantasy. I'm a very professional actress, so good at what I do that sometimes, men, when they're in a love scene with me, they forget that it's all for camera. You mustn't think or hope that –'

'And what about all that business you were up to with your hand?' he cries.

'Business?' she asks, perplexed.

'You know, fondling me!'

'Barry, love, I was only trying to give you a helping hand to calm you down . . .'

Her silk robe is flapping wide open top and bottom. Brian can't restrain himself any longer. He staggers over to her – walking still proving something of a challenge in his current on-going state. He pulls her to him and moves forward to kiss her.

'Er no,' she says quickly, turning her face sharply away, 'not that. We've already done that, haven't we?' she says. She just can't face any more of that mouth, she just can't. With the same hand that tortured him on set she now starts to undo his jeans – there's no time for much more messing about if she's going to make it to the boutique for that handbag before it closes.

Brian looks totally confused. Shock, terror, desire, now confusion – that's overdoing things a bit and he ends up just looking a bit daft which is a pity because he's not a bad-looking bloke on a good day. She removes his jeans then goes to recline invitingly on the little day bed in her dressing room. He stands hovering in his boxers. 'Come on then, get stuck in,' she says impatiently. (That handbag isn't going to wait forever.) Brian by now is past the point of trying to compute what is going on. He wonders whether he hasn't maybe died and gone to heaven or banged his head and had a dream that the gorgeous Serena Dawlish has just invited him to her dressing room and opened her legs for him. He tugs off his boxers and stumbles towards her. He tries to touch her but she tells him they don't need to bother with any of that either so he thrusts himself into her and starts to push.

Serena realises it's true what they say about men and their tongues.

At this point Serena's phone starts to ring. Serena sighs. She picks up the phone and looks at it. 'Omigod, it's Gareth! My manager!' she announces as if Moses were on the line. 'Don't worry, though, you carry on, Barry, love,' she commands as she takes the call. 'Hi Gareth. You need to see me? Urgently? Right. Actually can you hang on, no nothing, just had to move my leg a bit, it was getting pins and needles, that's all. Right, Gareth. So it's something urgent then, is it? Actually Gareth, can you hang on a sec again? Thanks, darling.' She puts her hand vaguely over the mobile and says to Brian, 'Can I tell you something?'

Jesus, Brian thinks. Could it be, could it be that this woman, this princess, this beauty is going to tell him she's in love with him?

'Tell me, tell me,' he pants.

'Could you push a bit harder please? Only I'm just not feeling very much at the moment.'

Brian's heart sinks. He's never had any complaints before – but then he's never been in a woman like Serena Dawlish before. Perhaps he's just not good enough for the likes of her.

Serena goes back to her phone call. 'Well, Gareth, if you're really sure it's that urgent . . .'

Brian redoubles his efforts, shoving himself harder and harder between her perfect honey golden thighs. He can feel the sweat of his exertions starting to seep back through the coating of powder on his face. He wants to come, he wants to come so badly but he mustn't, he mustn't. What would she think of him if he were to come so soon? God no, no, no, he mustn't come.

'OK, Gareth, if you say so,' she sighs underneath him.

Directly under Brian's face Serena's breasts are bouncing around like a pair of sumo wrestlers. He forces himself to look away. Whatever he does, he mustn't look there, no, he mustn't, he won't be able to hold back if he looks there so he looks at the wall and thinks about something awful like his mortgage or his team who are bottom of the league or anything to keep him going.

'Bye then,' says Serena to her manager. Abruptly she snaps shut her phone and equally precipitously pulls Brian out of her.

'What?' he cries, reeling.

'Listen, love, take a tip from a friend – you must learn to stop saying "what" all the time,' she tuts. 'It doesn't sound good.'

'Is something wrong?'

'Wrong? No.'

'But I haven't finished!'

'Haven't you? Well, I have, love. I told you – that was Gareth, my manager on the phone. You know what it's like when your manager clicks his fingers – you've got to run or they sulk.' She sighs as she dresses and runs her fingers through her hair to get the extensions back in their proper positions. 'It'll be some new promotional opportunity, I should expect, some supermarket that needs opening or some award I'm up for or something. It never ends. Do you find that – it never ends?' She looks at him standing in front of her, his trousers and boxers clinging to his knees. It certainly hasn't ended for Brian, she can see that much. She turns to go. 'See you on set next week then, Barry. I've got a couple of days off now.'

'It's Brian.'

'Sorry, yes, of course, Brian. Would you mind turning out the lights on your way out, please?'

'You're leaving? Just like that?' he whines, going pale under the orange.

'Yes – I told you, my manager wants to see me.'

'My God! Is that all I am to you – a quick screw?'

Serena tries to think of a politer way of saying yes.

'Because that's not all you are to me, Serena,' Brian wails. He flops in misery onto the day bed. Serena wishes he'd pulled his trousers up first – it's hardly polite otherwise. You never know with men how clean they are round the back.

'Can't you see I'm in love with you, Serena? I've been in love with you ever since I joined the cast of "Coombe Ridge Crescent". Even before that! I've got your poster on my bedroom wall. I want us to be together, Serena, together forever. Be a proper couple. Go public.'

Serena gasps and totters back, like one who has been assailed. 'Go public? Go public, you say? Are you crazy? I couldn't go public on a relationship just like that!'

'Because you're married, I understand . . .'

'No, no, not because of that. Because I'd need to talk to Gareth, look at my contract, work it into my schedule, discuss it with my sponsors! You have no idea!'

'But if you loved me, none of these things would matter,' Brian gasps.

'Look, it's lots of things, not just that you're called Brian and not just that you're only one of the junior members of the cast. It's, I don't know, everything. You've never won any awards, you don't promote any products,' she lists his failures out carefully on her immaculately manicured fingers, 'you've never been on a magazine cover, you . . . I could go on but what's the point? We have no future. That's all there is to it.'

She sees Brian's face crumple. It really doesn't suit him that expression; he doesn't want to get into the habit of pulling faces like that, she wants to tell him, but that's his manager's job, not hers, to give him advice like that.

'Don't be sad, Ba- Brian. If it's any consolation, love, you're not the first to be sitting there, crying, begging me for me. Some of this country's leading soap actors have been sat, lovesick and heart-broken, right where you are now,' she declares.

But at least they had the courtesy to pull their trousers up first, Serena thinks to herself as she closes the dressing room door behind her.

CHAPTER 3

Gareth is in his office contemplating the meeting he is about to have with Serena. It's not going to be easy. To say Serena is not bright is like saying the Grand Canyon is not small. She's a difficult bitch at the best of times. That tiresome mix of stroppy and ignorant. But he has to have this conversation, it's something that's got to be done. Gareth has enough experience in this game to know that when your clients start doing too well, that's when your skills really need to kick in. He's been biding his time and the moment is right now to unsettle her a little bit or, before he knows it, she'll be sniffing round for a new manager and his golden egg laying goose will be off. It's all happened before. Over the years he has learnt to protect his interests and stay one step ahead of the game. What matters is what's next; if you're dealing simply with what is you're already out of the loop. Yes, Serena is the most famous soap actress in Britain; yes, her appearance on a magazine cover sells God knows how many thousands of copies. Now is the time to bring her down a peg or two before she starts to realise there may be other opportunities out there for her.

It won't take much to destabilise her although he's going to have to choose his words carefully, nothing too strategic or she won't understand any of it. Serena doesn't really do concepts, only actions and words. And if things really don't work out he has another trick up his sleeve – Christine Cazale. He has taken her onto his books and he's trying to get her the part on 'Coombe Ridge Crescent' of Julie-Ann, Serena's long-lost younger sister who was separated from her at birth when they both got adopted by different families and who is now coming back from Australia after 23 years to live in Britain. If Serena does mess him about and leave him for another manager he'll hopefully have one of her best friends already signed up with him in a lead role on the show. That way he'll be covered whatever happens.

Gareth sits back in his black leather chair and reflects smugly on his prescience. Darwin would be proud of him.

*

Serena arrives at Gareth's office. He may be an ugly bastard but his offices are great, on the top floor of this big, tall, shiny building right near the shops in Bond Street. That's why she picked him, when she got the part on 'Coombe Ridge Crescent' and she had people lining up to represent her. She reckoned no one was going to be seeing her inside with him so it hardly mattered what he looked like, but there would be photographers outside and her highlights would look good against the pale pink marble of the entrance to the building.

And sure enough, as her driver opens her door and her long, longer, longest legs slide out, there's a gaggle of them there for her, gawping, jostling, just to get a photo of her going into her manager's office! God it's so embarrassing! Haven't these people got better things they could be doing?! There's wars out there, starvation, earthquakes, fashion shows and stuff, surely they're more important than just another photo of her?

Serena takes a deep breath because the complexion always looks best when you exhale (that's what her body coach has told her, anyway) – and then – wham, out she comes. The street lights up with watts and calls from the paps begging her to look their way or lift her skirt a little higher. Today, of course, as well as her face, body and hair Serena has another critical advantage; she has her shield, her armour, her ultimate weapon; she has her new handbag. Yes. She got to the shop just as the security guards were locking up but when she pressed her chest hard against the glass and they saw it was her, well . . . Their hands were trembling so much they could hardly grip hold of the keys to get the doors open for her again quickly enough. She is the first woman in Britain to have this handbag and the shop says they won't let anyone else have another one for a week, a whole week.

Serena wonders how much better life can get than to have this handbag, the most desirable, the most coveted, the most impossible to get hold of handbag in the country just for her, for a week. Not much better, she concludes; this is it, this is bliss. Serena has never been religious but as she clutches the handbag to her she feels very strong waves of something hard to describe. A sort of spiritual understanding of peace and inner global contentment waft through her. It is almost as if she is floating off onto a different ethereal dimension where she leaves all material concerns behind, all cares and preoccupations and just exists in a white, luminous space, her with her new handbag. She has heard of people having very intense emotional experiences like that and now she's having one too.

The cameras pop; Serena pouts. She hears someone cry, 'The handbag – she's got the handbag!' and suddenly her life feels spectacularly, hopelessly, unspeakably complete.

*

'Serena, I have good news and I have bad.'

Serena looks at him oddly. Bad? Bad? What makes him think she's paying him 12.75% of her earnings to hear news which is bad?

'OK,' she says. What she wants to say is, 'You do realise that there are a million other managers in London who would eat their hands off just to have a chance to have me on their books, don't you?' But she's feeling so good about her new handbag, so full of transcendental fulfilment and harmony that she can't really bring herself to care so all she says is, 'OK'.

He says, 'I'm going to give you the bad first.'

Now he's pushing it, he really is. The inner harmony suddenly doesn't feel quite so harmonious. 'May I give you the bad first?' or 'Would it be OK if I were to start with the bad?' – maybe. 'I'm going to give you the bad first' – I don't think so! He's getting over-confident, cocky – it always happens. To start off with they can't do enough to help you, then you start earning trillions for them and they begin to take you for granted. It's human nature and it's not very nice. She crosses her arms to show him, through her body language, that there is a high risk she is about to be not happy.

'Right,' she says.

'The point is, Serena, that you're not famous enough.'

Instantly Serena's shoulders drop. So – this has all been a wind-up, a laugh, a joke – not in the best of taste but there you go.

'God, you really had me going there, Gareth. For a minute there I thought you were being serious!'

'I am,' says Gareth, making a serious face to prove the point. 'You see, I've been in this business a long time,' he intones solemnly, 'and the fact is that today is not tomorrow.' He sees her puzzled expression and reminds himself that this is Serena and unless he keeps it simple he's wasting his breath. 'Look, what I'm saying is today, now, you are the star, at the top of your game, yes. But we have to look ahead. Although you are famous, very famous, the problem is that it's not quite the right quality of fame. It's not, I don't think, the sort of fame that's going to last.'

'So – this isn't a joke?'

'No.'

'So I'm not famous enough in the right sort of way?'

'That's it. That's it.'

Serena thinks hard. 'So, is what you're telling me, basically, you think I'm not good-looking enough? Because let me remind you, Gareth, that the readers of "Turn Me On" magazine, the widest read TV listings publication in the country have voted –'

'Yes, yes, I know that.'

'How can I look any better than what I already do?' she cries. 'Hair, tits, nose, arse, stomach, thighs, teeth, I've done it all. There's nothing else to change. There's nothing else I can do!'

'I'm not talking about looks, Serena.'

'What else is there?'

'You need to pierce the public consciousness in a different way.'

'What – like body piercings you mean?'

'No, that is not what I mean,' Gareth says patiently, slowing down so she can grasp the monosyllables more accurately. 'Look, Serena, you're 29, you're no spring chicken any more. There's new talent coming up all the time. You're getting on and you need to think about what you could do that makes you a bit different, what will preserve your fame and keep you famous but in a special, different kind of a way.'

Serena can see that Gareth really means what he's saying. At the best of times he's not much to look at but now his podgy face has gone all shiny with the effort of spelling it out to her. The impact of his words slowly sinks in. Not to be famous any more, the most famous of them all – her worst nightmare is now being presented to her, by her own manager! She feels a strange, cold panic ooze through her veins, almost as bad as the fear which washed over her when her surgeon told her that her blepharoplasty might have gone wrong. She stares at Gareth, her blue eyes wide, like two pools of sapphire plastic. What can she do? She'd wring her hands in despair only it would bugger up her nails. She racks her brain for inspiration.

'I could write my autobiography?' she says. 'You know, all about my childhood growing up in Gerrards Cross, going to brownies and girl guides, all the badges I did, how we found a dead squirrel in the garden once and –'

'I'm not sure about that,' Gareth interrupts her, shaking his head. 'We've tried the literary route and I don't really think it's for you, Serena. Your book "Gift Wrapping As A Hobby" didn't stay on the best-seller list for long.'

'What about depression – what if I had that? Because then

you can go to one of those clinics, can't you, and all it takes is a weekend and then you're out and cured and that's at least a double-page spread, isn't it?'

'A double page spread? That's not what we're talking about here! We're talking about total, permanent fame!'

'What about if I do another fitness DVD and wear even fewer clothes than last time?'

'Your last one only came out six weeks ago. No, I think it's going to take something more seminal.'

'Oh, you mean sex?'

'No, seminal – basic, fundamental. Somehow you just need to appear more real to the public.'

'Real? Of course I'm bloody real!'

'Reality is a relative not absolute commodity, Serena. Yes – you are real, but you don't want to be overtaken by others who are even more real than you, do you?'

'More real than me?'

'Yes. Now, being frank, you don't really have any other talents, do you? I mean, you can't sing, you can't dance . . . When it comes down to it you're a bit of a one trick pony, aren't you?

'Well, excuse me,' retorts Serena huffily, 'but when you're an actress dedicated to your craft you focus on that, you don't go poking around for other stuff, do you?'

'I suppose you could have a baby,' he shrugs.

'Baby!' Serena recoils, instinctively putting one hand over her expensive breasts and another over her even more expensive stomach. 'What? And ruin all the work I've had done on me?!'

Serena just can't think of anything she can do to improve on the package she already is. Every bit of her is already as good as it's ever going to get.

Gareth sighs and shrugs his shoulders again. 'It's not looking very good, is it?' he says mournfully.

'No,' Serena whispers. She starts fiddling nervously with

her wedding ring – and that's when it comes to her. James. She could get rid of him!

'There's always James, as a last resort,' she says.

'James?'

'Yes. James, my husband. We've been together four years now. Every mag has covered our perfect marriage in our lovely family home at least twice, there's just no more mileage in it. I could leave him! He's the greatest stage actor in Britain, that's got to be worth something?'

Gareth shakes his head. 'But that's just it, isn't it, Serena? He's this country's greatest stage actor. No one's going to be bothered about that, are they? Your fans couldn't give a toss about theatre. Your fans are proper people. They're not those arty-farty types who can afford fifty quid to sit in the South Bank and watch a drama about the psychology of the human condition, are they? Most of your fans won't even have heard of James Marlborough. He's not even their generation, is he? I mean he's so old now, what is he – almost 50?'

'Yes, well, just about, he's 43.'

'Right, well, there you go. You didn't have me managing you then otherwise I'd never have let you make such a promotionally unsuitable marriage,' Gareth comments. 'And, anyway, there's no question of you leaving him until you've got someone else lined up to replace him with. Can you imagine the headline – "Serena Dawlish, single and alone"? I don't think so! No, leaving James isn't enough. It's not enough to make you as famous as you need to be to keep your career alive.'

What is going on here? Serena wonders. She's had enough of this now. There's only so much negativity a girl can take in one day. All this gloomy talk is starting to get her down. Her career is more important to her than anything, she has to be famous, she has to. She doesn't like all the nasty stuff, she wants it to go away. Why doesn't Gareth sort it out, why doesn't he just tell her that he's made a mistake, everything's fine really. She needs to make him do that. Gareth's a man, isn't he? He may look like a toad but he's still a man. She can make any man respond to her charms, why can't that include him? She shuffles her shoulders around a bit to give her cleavage a better angle and moistens up her lips.

'Oh Gareth, Gareth,' she murmurs, 'you know how much I depend on you, you know how grateful I am to be in your hands.' She never thought it would come to this but needs must. As she says "hands" she reaches out and lightly touches Gareth's fingers with her own so he can make the connection more easily. She looks across at him and wills her pupils to dilate. She adjusts her breathing so it comes slow and steady, causing her chest to rise and fall, rise and fall with particular emphasis.

But Gareth's only response is a blank look and the merest hint of a sneer. She may be his most profitable client but she doesn't do it for him that way, not at all. He is immune to her charms. The kind of sex Gareth enjoys is something entirely different.

When she sees it's not working Serena suddenly snaps. 'Look, Gareth,' she fires back at him. 'You're the manager – you're the one who should be coming up with the ideas!'

'Right, well that's the good news – sort of. I have got three important things planned for you. For a start I've organised for you to do some charity work to develop a more caring profile.'

Serena pulls a face. 'Will it be with people who smell?' she asks. 'Only I can't do smells, I really can't, it's just a thing I have.'

Gareth feels his patience judder. 'No, no smells, Serena. And you're starting tomorrow morning. The opportunity came up and I grabbed it. It fits with your schedule, you don't have to be on set till the afternoon so that's not a problem.' He looks at her. 'Aren't you even going to ask what it is?'

'Well, I don't know, you said charity so I suppose it's what – handing out tins of food to old people or something?'

'No, it's teaching a literacy class to adults who can't read and write.'

'What – thick people?'

Not as thick as you, sweetheart, Gareth thinks to himself. 'No, not thick, just people who have missed the boat at school for whatever reason.'

'Aw, Gareth, what do you want to stick me with a bunch of saddos like that for? What good is that going to do?'

'A lot of good. Sue Upton is such a bitch. If you're not careful people will start to over-identify you with her and start to hate you for it.'

'OK,' mumbles Serena. She'd never thought of it that way.

'I've also found a slot for you in the first programme of a new prime-time TV show called "I Gave Birth To A Celebrity".'

'But I haven't given birth to anyone!'

'No, I know that,' Gareth replies slowly, 'but your mother has.'

'Don't be ridiculous! My mum's 53!'

'You,' Gareth explains through gritted teeth. 'Your mother gave birth to you.'

'Oh, so you mean the programme would be about me and my mum?'

Gareth reminds himself to breathe. 'Yes,' he says.

'Oh, that's good,' says Serena cheerfully. 'My mum's great. She's had prizes for her greengage jam. She does the church flowers, she chairs the church fête, she runs the church Bring and Buy every Wednesday and she's on the church fund-raising committee.'

'That'll wow them,' mutters Gareth. 'One of my secretaries has already rung her to tell her about the show. She's been sworn to secrecy and you also, Serena, must keep this to yourself. No one knows who the celebrity is, it's part of the contract. You can't show off to friends about it, can't tell the press, nothing. Not even your husband, James. The whole point of the show is the element of surprise. The audience won't know who they're seeing till he or she walks out on stage. Do you get that?'

'Of course I get it!'

'The show takes place the day after tomorrow so you don't have long to wait to keep quiet.'

'The day after tomorrow?!'

'This is the fast-moving world of television, Serena. We have to make sure we keep up. And frankly, my dear, given your situation, you've no time to lose.'

'OK, OK,' Serena moans, already bored with this subject. She's always on the telly – what difference is one more show going to make? 'And what's the third thing? You said you'd sorted three things for me.'

Yes, reflects Gareth. I was considering four, he tells himself, but I was concerned that would be a mathematical leap too far for you. 'That's right. The third thing is what you're going to like the most. I've signed you up as the face of Xerxes Carmen for the coming season.'

'Xerxes Carmen?' she shrieks. '*The* Xerxes Carmen, the fashion designer, the one who does all the fur and leather and stuff? Oh my God, Gareth, you are so amazing.'

'You get a whole free wardrobe of clothes which you have to wear.'

'Oh, like that's going to be hard!' she squeals.

'But I have to warn you, Serena – even with the charity work and the TV show and this clothes deal, I don't think it's going to be enough. I'm sorry, Serena, I really don't.'

'No, but it'll be a start, won't it?, and we can take it from there, can't we? Oh, a whole wardrobe of Xerxes Carmen clothes, I can hardly believe it!'

'It will be a start but I'm going to have to put in a lot of extra time for you, Serena, to really be able to support your career, to help you be properly famous. You understand that, don't you?'

'Oh, yes, and I am grateful.'

'So I've put together this new contract for you to sign which binds you to me for 5 years and increases my fee to 17.75% of all your income.'

'Oh, OK. So like, on the money I get for doing this TV show, I pay you 17.75% of it?'

'Sort of. You pay me 17.75% of what you would be earning as recognition of my expertise in finding and setting up the show for you but we actually log your hypothetical earnings from it on your accounts as a promotional zero earning scenario and you actually pay me from your regular income on "Coombe Ridge Crescent". Are you with me?'

'Whatever, Gareth,' Serena mumbles, bored with all this. 'When will the clothes be delivered?'

'In the morning.'

'What? Tomorrow morning! Oh my God! I can't wait!'

'You just sign the new contract here. That's it. Well done.'

'How will they know my dress size?'

'Don't you worry, I've taken care of all of that.'

'Oh Gareth, you are a babe, you really are.'

'There's one last thing – we need to talk about how you're going to wear the clothes.'

'Oh Gareth,' says Serena, 'I do know how to put clothes on! I'm not stupid, you know.'

Hush my mouth, thinks Gareth.

'Actually the agreement is fairly complex. For example, not only do you have to wear the clothes but you have to be seen with the XC logo visible at all time. So you should take this and make sure you wear it in a prominent place whenever you go out.' He hands her a silver brooch with the initials XC intertwined.

'What is it?'

Gareth takes another deep breath. 'It's a brooch.'

'No, I mean, is it silver? White gold? Platinum?'

'I've no idea. And it hardly matters what the content is, it's what it looks like that counts. The important thing is, it has to be visible on you at all times, aside from when you're on set, of course, otherwise they start taking money off your fee, do you get that?'

'Sure,' Serena sniffs.

'Right. So you get the picture – they have the exclusive.'

'Yeah, yeah, I know,' says Serena, getting bored. 'Xerxes Carmen is a very exclusive name, you don't have to tell me that.'

'No, I mean exclusive in that you can only ever wear Xerxes Carmen clothes and accessories.'

'Well, they'd better send me plenty of stuff then!'

'They will, don't worry. Now the arrangement starts immediately so I've got one outfit here for you, you can get changed into that now, and all the rest will be delivered to your house tomorrow.'

'Oh Gareth, you're so good to me,' Serena burbles grabbing hold of the new clothes. She runs into the loo to change and reappears, swathed head to toe in tasselled leather. 'It's divine,' she crows, 'just fab fab fab!'

'I'm glad you like it. Now for the accessories – these boots and this bag.'

'Right. Great boots but I've got a new bag already thanks.'

'No, I'm sorry, I've told you. Xerxes Carmen have the exclusive. The other handbag has to go.'

All the blood drains away from Serena's face. She backs slowly away from him, clutching the bag ever closer to her, letting out a sharp high-pitched wail of mammalian distress. 'No, Gareth, no! Don't do that to me! Not the handbag. Don't take it away from me! Please, please, no!'

He looks at her. 'Serena, you've got no choice. It has come to this. You have this opportunity and you must take it. I've explained it all to you. I thought you'd understood. You must do this. Your fame is too ephemeral.'

'F-ing what?'

'Ephemeral. It means that everything changes, nothing stays the same. Your future is at stake, don't you see? These lifelines I've arranged for you – the charity work, the TV show, the clothes deal – they're your only hope! We're talking last chance saloon here! You're 29 – your glory days are about to be over! Take these last crumbs of hope I'm offering you before they too are blown away and you are left with nothing!'

Serena gives up. She empties out the contents of the donkey skin handbag and puts them in the Xerxes Carmen one. She hands the donkey skin handbag over to Gareth. She manages to fight back the tears until she has stomped out of his office past the posse of flashing cameras and back to the safety of her waiting BMW where she would cry her heart out except it would mess up her mascara for the photographers waiting for her when she gets home.

CHAPTER 4

The second Serena is out of Gareth's office there's only one thing she wants to do and that is what every woman wants to do when her life fails to follow the story-line – pour her heart out to her best friend. Serena's best friend is Christine Cazale. Christine has been Serena's best friend since Thursday when Serena had a bust-up with her previous best friend, the actress from the soap 'Drummond's Drive', Holly Diamond. They had a stand-up fight in a restaurant about exfoliation which not only ended up with Holly ruining one of Serena's favourite dresses when she threw red wine over it, the slag, but worse than that, the argument didn't even appear in any of the mags. Serena and Holly offered to re-stage it for photographers the next day but no one took them up on it.

Christine is another actress who is not as famous as Serena (of course). Poor Christine has been going through a terrible time of it. For a start she has recently tried getting back with her ex-husband. Both of them had careers in nose-dive and reckoned it was worth a try, two heads being better than one and all that, but as it turned out no one seemed much bothered whether they were together or not so they separated again. Then, as if that wasn't bad enough, the last time she had her colour done it went wrong and when she went back to have it re-done big tufts of her hair started falling out and the extensions they put in to cover the gaps were rubbish and didn't take. The final straw came when she developed some weird calcium deficiency in her nails and they started splitting and going all flaky and her beautician said the only thing for it was for Christine not to wear varnish for a whole month to give her nails a chance to recover.

Christine is such a dear, sweet friend and the fact that

however bad Serena's problems are Christine's are always worse is such a comfort.

They arrange to meet immediately for a drink in a fashionable bar in Sloane Street in the hope that, while they talk, someone significant will notice them and take their photo.

'So, Christine,' Serena begins earnestly, 'tell me all about you.'

Christine starts to witter on in the background about her audition with Mark Turnbull-Ash, the producer of 'Coombe Ridge Crescent', for the role of Julie-Ann. Meanwhile Serena takes out her mobile phone so she can use the time to send a few texts. Listening to other people's problems isn't really Serena's thing. When she's done with that she starts to think about whether she should confide in Christine, her new best friend, about what Gareth has said to her about Serena not being quite famous enough. Christine will reassure her that what Gareth has said is crap, that Serena is fantastic, the best in the business and always will be, and that will be so good to hear.

'So what do you think, do I have a chance of getting it?' Christine asks. 'Serena?'

'Sorry what was that, lovey?' Serena replies affectionately.

'Do you think I've got any chance with Mark?' Christine repeats.

Serena stares at her. Should she tell her what Gareth has said or not?

'Are you OK, babe?' Christine enquires tenderly. Serena isn't looking quite herself this evening.

'Sort of.'

'You know what, Serry, your extensions are looking so good at the moment. Really, really good.'

'Thanks, love.'

'And your clothes and your make-up, they're all so, so great, really coordinating.'

'Thanks, Chris, but – you know, there's more to life than hair and clothes and make-up and everything.'

Now Christine is worried. Now Serena is sounding slightly delirious. 'Are you feeling all right, darling? Not running a bit of a temperature or something?'

Serena shakes her head. 'It's just that life is so ephemereal, don't you think?'

Christine goes pale. Now Serena's talking in tongues. She's heard about this kind of thing happening to people who are too successful and just can't cope with the stress of it all.

'I'm not really getting you, Serena. This afternoon you texted me to tell me you'd got your new donkey skin handbag. You said you were over the moon, that you couldn't have been happier, that now you had that handbag your life was complete. And I was so, so happy for you, I really was. Where is it, by the way – is that it? That's not it! That's not donkey skin! That's a Xerxes Carmen bag. They're good, aren't they? I've got one of those. Anyway you said you didn't see how you could ever possibly be unhappy again – it was the longest text you've ever sent me!'

'Yes! Yes! I was happy, happier than I've ever been, I did get that handbag and I really felt my life had entered a new dimension – but then it happened!'

'What?' cries Christina, aghast, as aghast as the Botox will let her do aghast anyway. 'What happened, Serry?'

Serena's about to tell her what Gareth has said, she wants to share her pain, she wants to hear someone, anyone say that it's not true and that Serena is amazing, that she's going to be at the top of her game forever but at the last moment she stops herself. Admission of even minor failings, much less this kind of trauma, is just not good for the image.

'Gareth told me I had an exclusive deal with Xerxes Carmen, clothes and accessories, and that I had to give him back the donkey skin handbag.'

The champagne flute starts to shake in Christine's spray-tanned hand. 'What? Your new handbag? But you've got the only one in the country for a whole week!'

'How do you know that?'

'Cos I rang to see if I, like, could have one too and they said you had it for a week and when I said I was a friend of yours, actually your best friend, they said OK, I could have the first one after you at the end of the week but not before then. God, Serry, you must be gutted!'

'I am.'

'I mean, like, yeh, it's great to have the Xerxes Carmen deal and everything but the donkey skin handbag! My God. To think – you had it, you held it in your hands, for a few precious moments it was yours – and then it was taken from you. It was gone. It must feel like, well, it must feel a bit like death really.'

'Yes,' Serena agrees miserably.

'Is there anything, anything I can do to help?'

'No. Thanks. There's nothing,' Serena resolves bitterly.

'Aw, Serry, love, it must be horrible for you. I'm so, so sorry,' Christine commiserates, reaching out to squeeze her hand.

'That's OK,' Serena sniffs, snatching her hand back (you never know – that nail thing might be infectious and, sorry, but there are some risks Serena just can't afford to take).

'To think that you've got that upset to deal with while that bitch Holly Diamond is going round slagging you off all the time!'

'Oh, I don't worry what she says. It's all crap. No one takes what she says seriously. She's only bitter because she's not my best friend any more.'

Christine nods unconvincingly. 'Sure, Serry.'

'So what's she saying about me now?'

'Oh, you know, like you say, it's all crap.'

'Yeh, but what kind of crap?'

Christine squirms slightly in her seat and makes an uncomfortable face. 'It's nothing, Serry, nothing.'

'What is it, Chris? There's something you're not telling me, isn't there?'

'No, babe, it's nothing, nothing really.'
'Tell me!'
'No, really, it's –'
'Christine, you've got to tell me. We're best mates now, aren't we? I tell you everything, don't I? What about that day when I noticed your silk dress had damp patches running down either side at the armpits just as we were about to go into the Annual National Television Awards Ceremony! And what about your nasal hair? I've been up front with you on everything – the very least you owe me is to be as honest with me!'

'OK,' says Christine, taking a deep breath, 'If you really, really want to know.'

'Yes!'

'Well – she thinks you've got funny eyebrows.'

'Funny eyebrows?'

'Yeh.'

Serena immediately whips out a mirror from her handbag and starts inspecting her face.

'Funny in what way?' she asks desperately.

'Well, she says low. She says they're too low.'

'Omigod!' Serena presses her face ever closer to the mirror. 'What do you think, Christine?'

'What do I think?' Christine stammers.

'Yes! You! What do you think?' Serena cries.

'It wasn't me who said it!' Christine pleads. 'It doesn't matter what I think!'

'Tell me!' Serena yells back at her.

'Well, you know what they say – the eyebrows really do frame the face and yours are –'

'Well?!'

'Well,' Christine blubbers, wondering why she ever started this, 'perhaps they are just a tiny bit low . . .'

'What – both of them? Or just one side more than the other?'

'It's not so much one or the other. It's more like bits of both and not bits of both.'

'I don't understand,' Serena whimpers, trembling. 'Low how?'

'OK, well, the bits near your nose are OK, I suppose, a bit too far apart but I don't think it's really that. What it really is, is the bits the other end which should go high, shouldn't they, to sort of like open up the face? Whereas yours just go straight across, they stay too low.'

'Show me!'

'Well,' Christine gulps, 'yours look a bit like this,' and here she makes an impression of cro-magnon man, 'when they would look so much better a bit more like this' and here she lifts the skin at the end of either eye to effect the look of someone who has just had a rectal examination. She sees Serena's expression of horror. 'Look, babe, I'm only trying to help . . .'

Serena is lost for words. Who the fuck does this woman think she is? This woman whose last appearance on TV was three months ago in that daft hospital drama as the nurse who gets sacked for using a dead patient's credit card, who does she think she is giving her, Serena Dawlish, lectures about her face? Has she looked at her own recently? That botched nose job with a tip that sticks out so far you could rest a tea cup on it; the teeth that look like they were designed to crack nuts; the upper arms so flabby she could probably take off with them if she flapped them hard enough – what about them? Does Serena ever have a go at her about them?

'Can I just remind you, Christine – it's me who's a top soap star, me who's been voted for three years running now "The Most Attractive Woman In A Soap" by the readers of "Turn Me On" magazine, me who's appearing the day after tomorrow on . . .'

'On what?'

'On . . . on . . . the cover of "Woah!" magazine. So my

eyebrows can't be that bloody bad, can they?' With this Serena puts on her Xerxes Carmen coat, picks up her new Xerxes Carmen handbag, turns the side with the XC brooch on it to the front like she's been told to, and stands to go.

'You did ask, Serry. You did ask me to tell you!'

'I'm sorry, Christine, but this time you've overstepped the mark!' Serena cries and turns on her Xerxes Carmen heel to leave, because she's good at storming-out scenes.

Except that, as the four inch heel pivots on the floor, there's something about this particular scene and her last line in it that doesn't feel quite right. No, not right at all. What was it she has just said – 'overstep the mark'? And what was it Christine had said to her at the beginning of their conversation? – 'Do you think I've got any chance with Mark?'

Serena stops in mid-storm-out and rewinds.

'What you were saying before, about Mark – you didn't mean Mark Turnbull-Ash, the producer of "Coombe Ridge Crescent", did you?'

'Well of course I did. I've already told you, told you everything! Weren't you listening to anything I was saying?'

Frankly, Serena was not so now Christine has to tell it to her all over again.

*

'*O, reason not the need; our basest beggars*

Are in the poorest thing superfluous.'

It's late. James is in his study watching the DVD of his last rehearsal; he likes to have them all filmed so he can watch himself afterwards and see how good he is.

'*Allow not nature more than nature needs,*

Man's life's as cheap as beast's.

But, for true need –

You heavens, give me that patience, patience I need!'

To think of what he had been in his youth – the public school boy gone bad, the dissolute, delinquent Jimmy, thieving, drinking, shagging girls on a whim, for a joke, for a laugh, for a dare, for a bet. To think how he has reinvented himself from that wayward wastrel to the magnificent James Marlborough of today. Yes, when he discovered his talent for acting, he found his metier.

'*You see me here, you gods, a poor old man,*
As full of grief as age; wretched in both!'
                              You think I'll weep;
No, I'll not weep.
I have full cause of weeping; but this heart
shall break into a hundred thousand flaws,
Or ere I'll weep. O fool, I shall go mad!'

My God, how wonderfully he delivers these lines! And the detail of his movement – everything is splendid. The boldness of his eye, the fluidity of his breath reinforcing the vigour of his stated intent, the arrogance of his pose bearing witness to the nobility of his lineage, with only the set of his chin hinting at the imminent carnage. It is all sublime, sublime. No wonder Geraldine can't resist him when he recites: he feels like coming himself when he watches himself in action.

★

It's time for bed. Serena applies another coat of lipstick to her soft, full lips. She admires her features in her bedroom mirror. She really is gorgeous. Actually gorgeous isn't the right word, she reflects – it's more stunning than simply gorgeous. Last night she felt gorgeous but tonight she definitely feels more stunning than gorgeous. Sort of like still gorgeous but sort of stunning as well as and on top of being gorgeous. Then suddenly something isn't right. Something isn't perfect. All at once she remembers what Christine said earlier about her eyebrows.

Jesus, the eyebrows!

Are they low?

She lifts them a bit, then a lot, then hardly at all – but there is no escaping the truth: her eyebrows really are a couple of millimetres lower than they should ideally be. Panic grips her.

Christine was right. Serena has got amazing eyes, large, lovely, turquoise blue eyes, but unless she holds them slightly wider open than they would naturally be, unless she lifts her eyebrows just a touch, her eyes look a bit too deep-set and it spoils everything else in her face.

How can she have looked at her face as often as she has done all these years and not seen this before?

She realises that she really ought to have immediate surgery on them but how can she? Now she's so successful the soap depends on her. Without single mother of three Susan Depton in every other scene 'Coombe Ridge Crescent' would grind to a halt. When she tried going on holiday to Ibiza last year with some girlfriends for a fortnight the ratings plummeted and now the producer has pretty much told her to put the rest of her life on hold.

She practises again: she opens her eyes a bit wider – no, that's no good. A bit less – God no! There's a just perfect ratio of eyelid to eyebrow she needs to achieve. She practises it in front of the mirror and then away from it and then back in it again to see if she's managed to hold it. For now she has, thank God, for the moment she has. What if, as a next step, she were to try walking downstairs to talk to her husband, James, have an entire conversation with him, and then come back, upstairs, into the bedroom and see if she can hold her eyes wide like this through all of that? What if she were to try that? It's a bit of a gamble. But she feels, for professional artistic reasons, she ought to give it a go. Yes, what the hell, she'll do it. One last look in the mirror then down she goes, down, down, all the way downstairs to where James is sitting learning his lines in his study. He won't like being disturbed but it's too bad – she has to get this right before she films her big wedding scene where she secretly gets engaged to her stepfather's sister's ex-fiancé only to find out he is father to her best friend's daughter's baby.

She enters the room. She waits for James to look up.

'Hello, Serena,' he murmurs wearily.

She stands and says nothing. Will he notice her new facial arrangement? Has she managed to hold it all the way downstairs?

'What is it?' he asks.

'Nothing, just sort of hi, how's it going?'

'Jesus, Serena, how many times have I told you I won't be disturbed when I'm learning my lines!'

Serena wonders whether she can sit down and hold the eyes. She stares at the sofa and calculates the obstacles.

'I mean, really, come on, you know what it's like for me when I'm doing my lines. And this is Lear, Serena, Lear, for Christ's sake!'

What Serena really wants at this stage is a mirror. What she wouldn't give for a mirror. Why doesn't James keep a mirror in his study? She's sitting down now but she's pretty sure, she really is, that she's kept them wide open, just wide enough, not too much. She gets so excited that she feels her forehead start to relax involuntarily back into a normal position and it takes every ounce of her professional will to keep the wretched thing high enough to lift the brows to lift the eyes to keep the whole show in place.

'Anyway, now you're here, now I've been disturbed, shall I run you through some of it? You don't know the play, do you?'

Serena gives him a look to show him how daft he is even to ask. Undeterred, James stands up and positions himself. His stomach protrudes and hangs, like a second head, looming over the top of his trousers. He's undone the zip to make himself more comfortable – horrible. The bags under his eyes are heavy and grey. She knows, from experience, that if she says anything, if she makes any criticism or comment about his appearance and says he ought to make more of an effort to look smart at home, he'll tell her what the hell, he's relaxing in his own house, he's won six Oliviers, his stomach can do what the fuck it likes. But Serena just doesn't see it that way. They're both professional actors. They've got to think about their fans, about their public, whenever, whatever, even when no one can see them. You can't have it both ways, you just can't!

Why on earth had she ever married him? Why hadn't she had more faith in herself? Everyone had always told her she was going to be successful – her mum, her psychic, her tap dance teacher. If only she'd listened to her own inner voice and the advice of others! If only she'd learnt to hold her eyes open wider sooner! Now, at 29, she's a major star in a soap with higher ratings than anything else on prime-time TV. He's a middle-aged stage actor spouting up stuff written by some bloke five hundred years ago, stuff no one can make any sense of anyway and she's lumbered with him, well and truly lumbered! James clears his throat and gets ready to recite.

'To 't, luxury, pell-mell! for I lack soldiers.

Behold yond simpering dame, Whose face between her forks presages snow;

That mines virtue, and does shake the head

To hear of pleasure's name;'

What the fuck is he on about? Frankly Serena has never understood what it is people see in Shakespeare. It's not real, is it?, it's not how people really speak, so what's the point of it? On her soap, people talk the way people really talk and do what they really do. If Shakespeare's so bloody good why can't someone rewrite it into normal, modern language? All those weird words; all those silly, far-fetched plots – you've got to keep your story-line credible or you lose your viewers overnight, everyone knows that. And as for James, Jesus Christ, if only he could see himself as he truly is – 43 – old, old, old, old, old. Old. Shapeless. Hairless. But none of this matters any more – what does matter is that she has kept her eyebrows in the right place. She stands, ready to make her triumphant return up the stairs to the bedroom mirror for final and total verification of her victory.

'The fitchew, nor the soiled horse, goes to 't
With a more riotous appetite . . .

– where are you going?!' James cries after her. 'Serena! Where are you going! Stop! Wait! I'm right in the middle of my soliloquy!'

Serena, however, is already gliding up the stairs. She is this country's leading TV actress. She earns more in one episode of 'Coombe Ridge Crescent' than James does in an entire week on stage every night. She does not know what a sollylocky is and she couldn't give a shit.

She gets to the bedroom and looks – yes! Yes! Perfect, perfect! Her eyes are wonderfully exactly open, wide but not too wide. A wave of pure pleasure explodes in her chest, the sheer unadulterated joy of physical achievement.

Moments later James appears, lurking in the doorway. She sees him standing, staring, behind her in the mirror.

The fact is that James is still suffering from the after-effects of seeing Geraldine at lunch with a rabid erection that will not go away. His dick, still cock-a-hoop, feels like it's got a size 4 sock on a size 8 foot – an agony of suppression. Although the sight of his wife in her vulgar red embroidered kimono, with her grotesquely inflated breasts and her artificial hair, is fundamentally revolting to him she is, after all, a woman and, what's more, a woman who is his wife and therefore available to him so she'll have to do for now. As long as he doesn't look at her face he'll be fine.

What's more, if he's going to dump Geraldine, as he has every intention of doing once she is over her histrionic reaction to his decision, he has to get used to sex with Serena again. He hasn't bothered to service her for months. There's been no need. Since he started the relationship with Geraldine he hasn't really required any topping-up in between visits to her flat; just rest really. But Lear doesn't open for another

3 weeks so until he has seduced the rather lovely young actress who will be playing Cordelia in that someone has to fill the gap and a wife is so convenient.

Anyway, when all is said and done, James has got to make his marriage work. The alternative is too financially horrible to contemplate.

'What do you want?' Serena snaps at him.

Sex, James would like to say. Quick, functional sex. But of course that message is going to require a spot of paraphrasing if he's going to make it happen. James has learnt, over the years, that the only communication his wife responds to is flattery. As long as he tells her she looks good first he's in there.

'I've just come up to say how wonderful you're looking today,' he says flatly. 'Wonderful. You always look wonderful but today, now, downstairs, just now, more wonderful than ever.'

Yes, Serena thinks smugly. I do, I do, and I know why. She sees the longing and desire in James face. That's when it comes to her. Of course! Sexual intercourse would put her ability to maintain her optimum eyebrow height to the ultimate test!

They haven't done it for ages – Serena had kind of thought that James was probably past all that kind of thing now he's 43 but maybe there was a bit of life in the old dog yet. Not that she even remotely fancies him any more, and she gets plenty from her various affairs with men in the soap, but a quick one-off now just to see if she really can make this eyebrow thing work would be worth it.

To speed things up Serena goes and lies down on the bed and starts massaging her chest. She did this in a recent episode of 'Coombe Ridge Crescent', the one where she'd been kidnapped from the Crescent and held prisoner for ten days with no food or water in full make-up by an ex-boyfriend in a lighthouse on the south coast. Serena had complained that she didn't understand why it had to be a lighthouse, what was wrong with a shopping mall or a luxury hotel, couldn't she be held prisoner there? Her director, Terry, said it had to be a lighthouse, people would get the metaphor but Serena didn't so why would anyone else? Anyway, when he came to rescue her, her new boyfriend had to run up 356 steps to get to her. The director said, 'He's run up 356 steps to get to you, darling. Make it worth his while. Run your hand across your tits and tell him you want him to take you now, by the light of the moon and the stars, take you until there is no more breath in your body.' So Serena had duly run her hand across her tits and told the poor bloke she wanted him to take her by the light of the moon and the stars until there was no more breath in her body. Unfortunately, after the 356 steps, there was already no more in his and they'd had to cut the scene to wait for him to recover enough to be able to stand upright much less take advantage of Sue's kind offer. Nevertheless, grown men all over Britain had apparently swooned in their sitting rooms when they saw Serena fondling herself in this way and the media people bumped up the price of ads in the next 4 episodes of the programme by 45%.

'Take me now, by the light of the moon and the stars,' Serena repeats again now, because she wants James to hurry up and get on with it so she can check her eyes as soon as it's over and because regurgitating other people's lines is always so much less hassle than having to invent her own.

James knows they're lines from her soap and she knows James knows. So what.

Without any further encouragement she has moved to the bed and parted her legs. Strangely, given their long abstinence from each other, she seems as keen for sex as he is. She must have been desperate for him all these months, the poor woman, desperate. James feels his penis surging impatiently forth from his striped Y fronts. He needs to get inside her quick as poss. If she says anything else inevitably it will be something stupid in that inane, grating voice of hers and it will put him off. Or if he looks too closely at her face, at those absurd dolly's painted features, he will lose it, he knows from experience he will.

For some reason, as she lies there, she is holding her eyes wide open in a peculiar way as if preparing for an audition for a part as one of the waking dead. He considers whether he should enquire politely after this then checks himself – what does he care if her eyeballs look as if she's on steroids, it's not her eyes he's after.

'Take me until there is no more breath in my body,' Serena cries again.

Fuck that, thinks James, all I want is a quick shag to shake off this erection.

As his trousers are still undone he simply has to shake his hips to let them drop. This is an effective but not necessarily attractive action on a man as well-padded as James. Serena hopes and prays that he's at least going to keep on the baggy and shapeless T-shirt to cover up the baggy and shapeless stomach. That way she can always fantasise that he has a tanned, toned six pack underneath and not the hairy bulge that lurks there.

James starts to take off his T-shirt.

'No, it's OK,' she says quickly. 'You can keep that on.'

James shrugs his shoulders and begins to peel off his Y-fronts instead. When he has done this he stands for a moment before mounting her, all the better for her to appreciate the size of his mammoth member.

Serena is starting to lose interest. This is taking forever and she can't hold this eye position thingy for ever. She looks across to see how he's getting on. For some reason he's just standing there with his little tadger flapping between his skinny white thighs.

It makes Barry's earthworm look like the Loch Ness Monster.

'Get on with it then,' she says.

Jesus. Why did she have to speak again? That cheap, bland voice of hers. For a man as attuned to vocal excellence as James that voice is hell. He won't even try kissing her – the last time he'd bothered doing that there was so much red smeared all round his mouth afterwards he looked like he'd bitten the head off a kitten. So instead he lies on top of her and starts nuzzling her neck with his nose.

But the last thing Serena wants if she's going to get through this whole thing with her eyes open just to the right degree is for her head to be knocked this way and that with James' soppy, sloppy attempts at kisses and all his hot dribble running down her neck.

'I told you,' she repeats, 'just get on with it.'

That voice again. The raucous fishwife's voice. James can feel his erection losing faith, losing hope, losing interest. Please God no, he thinks, please no!

He tries pushing himself up into her but it's too late, too late. She has spoken, he has heard and he cannot, he cannot penetrate a woman whose vocal timbre has the harmonic content of a skidding tyre. But if he gives up now he'll only be in a worse state than ever in half an hour's time. He knows his cock. It will not be thwarted. It was roused then abandoned at lunch time. It does not have the psychological resources to take a second rejection. He has to get it in, get it done now. He has to.

'You're not very hard are you?' she complains, reaching down and manually inspecting his goods. 'How can we have sex with that? For us to have sex you need a proper hard-on and you could use many words to describe this but hard isn't one of them.'

'Maybe not rock hard, no. It's a semi. There's hope.'

'A semi? Semi what? Semi-detached, semi-skimmed? Semi what?'

'Just a semi – half way there! All it needs is a bit more

cosseting from a woman who acts like she means it,' he mumbles bitterly.

Serena's got her eyes shut. He doubts it's ecstasy. He just can't get his bloody thing to go stiff enough to get in. All he can do is prod her with his hopelessly supine member which feels like trying to spear a jellyfish with an eel.

Fuck this for a lark, his dick complains, wilting ever further.

Serena sits up and looks for her cigarettes.

'What are you doing?'

'Getting a ciggy.'

'But we're not done yet! We've only just started!'

'Why don't we just face facts? We haven't done it for months and you haven't got a proper hard-on now. It must just be a –'

'A what?'

'Well, you know, an age thing. There's no point stressing. Just accept it. Go with the flow. Take up golf, go on a cruise, you know, do what people your age do instead.'

'An age thing? I'm 43!'

'Exactly.'

'I'm fine, I'm fine,' James gasps in exasperation. 'Just put – put your hand back on him, talk to him, give him some encouragement!'

Serena has never got into this whole talking-to-the-penis thing that men seem so keen on. It seems, well, ridiculous to her. It would never occur to her to ask a man to talk to her clitoris. Nevertheless, for the purposes of the experiment she tries to show goodwill. She lies down again and gropes around between his legs, her hand having to reach ever higher before she eventually locates the damp, shrivelled squib of skin that is now James' manhood.

'Um, to be honest,' she begins, although stating the obvious has always been a pet hate of hers, 'I think that it – he – has lost interest.' Just like me, she thinks.

'No, no!' James insists.

They both look down at the inert blob lying grey and flaccid in her pretty pink palm. The proud tattoo of his youth, the wording "CARPE DIEM" inscribed the length of his member, has shrunk to a slightly less magnificent "CAD".

'Um, I think it has.'

'Talk to him! Talk to him!' James implores.

'Oh God – um, hello, er dick, dickie. Come on, be a nice dickie boy, um, be a nice hard dickie, a nice big dickie stiffy thingy, um . . .'

James wants to weep with frustration. 'Not like that! Tell him you want him! Tell him you love him. Make him think he's the most wonderful penis you've ever seen!!'

Blimey, thinks Serena, that'll require a bit of imagination 'Er, ooh you wonderful dick thing, in all the universe there cannot be a dick as wonderful as you, not on the moon, or in Jupiter, or Mars, or – what's that other one? The one they always make the joke about, the anus thingy one, what was it? . . .'

James' virility has frazzled to the size and consistency of one of those goldfish you win at a funfair, the sort that's dead in its little see-through plastic bag even before you get it home.

'Maybe if you took it in your mouth –' he suggests lamely, but one look at Serena and he can tell he hasn't got a hope in hell of that.

'I'm tired, I've had enough,' she groans. She gets up, fag in hand, still holding her forehead high, and goes and peers at herself in the mirror. The moment she removes her body from his the erection bounces back. He hits it so hard in irritation he almost knocks it off.

Serena stubs out the cigarette and goes into the bathroom. She has a pee and starts to brush her perfect white teeth while she looks at her reflection in the mirror. Bloody hell. All that hassle and yet she's still managed to keep the new eyebrow hold.

She amazes even herself.

Then she notices that by lifting her eyebrows like that all the time she's bringing on frown lines on her forehead! That Christine Cazale, the bitch! She must have known that when she suggested it to her! She wanted her to get a prematurely wrinkled forehead!

She immediately drops her eyebrows.

She's so fed-up. She's fallen out with her old best friend; she can't trust her new best friend; her manager is telling her she's not famous enough and she's stuck with this old fart of a husband who can't even get it up. She could have any man anywhere and she's got him. He never appears in any magazines, the only famous people he knows are stage actors and they don't really count. Everyone thinks she must be deliriously happy. She knows that this is probably because she keeps telling everyone in magazine interviews that she is deliriously happy with her husband, her house, her career, but she only says that because Gareth told her it's what you've got to say, no one wants a sob story unless it's in the past tense he told her, and this is present, this is very present.

She thinks how she'd give anything for a good screw to release all her frustrations. Sex with Barry or whatever he was called earlier in the day had been so useless it had been a relief to have Gareth's call interrupting it. And there was no point going back out to try again with that old fool of a husband, they'd only go through the whole ordeal again and she'd be left feeling worse than ever.

She remembers the love scene they filmed today. If only love really could be like that! Romantic and passionate! She remembers her kissing noises. God those noises are good. She makes them again now for herself in front of the mirror. She thinks how wonderful it would be if she could make that kind of noise about someone and really mean it.

★

Geraldine is about to go to bed when she decides she doesn't believe what James has told her. About not having sex with his wife. And once she gets the doubt in her head she knows she will not sleep until she has verified the facts. It's simply the kind of woman she is. So she gets in her car, tucks Beckett into the passenger seat next to her on his velvet pillow and sets off from Islington for Brentford.

It's a crazy idea but this is Geraldine after all. She read a lot of the Theatre of the Absurd in her formative years and these things leave their mark.

James lives in The Butts, a delightful enclave of Georgian properties in Brentford. The moment she arrives at his house and opens the car door all she can hear are the strident tones of that bloody Serena crying out through the open bedroom window, 'Take me now, by the light of the moon and the stars! Take me until there is no more breath in my body!'

So she was right. She knew it. The bastard! The lying, cheating bastard! For a while she stands, shaking, on the pavement, too incensed to know what to do next. Then, after several minutes, she hears more groaning noises, this time from the en-suite bathroom. They've gone in there for a second go! All at once Geraldine's mind is made up. She's going to climb up there, appear at the window and catch James in flagrante!

The front of the elegant façade of James' house is smothered in a rich, dripping wisteria. Geraldine sets up the camera function on her mobile so it's all ready once she's up there then starts the journey north up towards his bedroom window, inching her way in her Manolo Blahniks along the wisteria bough which is not as solid as it looks from the pavement. As she moves precariously onwards and upwards the bough gapes and creaks and heaves. Her hand-embroidered vintage Indian cashmere shawl keeps getting caught on its branches. The higher she climbs the more the wisteria pulls and strains, even against Geraldine's minimalist form. Reason tells Geraldine to turn round and climb down but then Reason never has been Geraldine's strong point.

*

James is hovering anxiously outside the bathroom door. The thing is, he's sure if he had another shot at it, he'd keep it up. It's full-on now, he has a fine, stout flagpole an eighteen year old would be proud of. If she'd just let him have another go he could do it. He tries to find the right formulation of words to whisper through the door to her to get her back in position. What does one say to one's wife in these circumstances?

'Listen, I think I might be ready for another crack at it?'

'Look, he's back on form so can I get back on you?'

Nothing seems quite right. Just as he's struggling with the right vocabulary and syntax he hears noises coming from the other side of the door. Groaning, moaning noises.

Serena is bringing herself off in there!

God – first Geraldine at lunch, now Serena. He really does drive women mad with desire for him. What a stud he is!

If she's that keen he decides to forego the niceties. He rips open the door, pins Serena up against the bathroom wall and thrusts himself against her. Weirdly, she's got a mouth full of toothpaste. What sort of a woman masturbates and brushes her teeth at the same time? But this is the least of his worries. The moment he is face to face with those large popping blue eyes, wide with surprise, expectation and stupidity then instantaneously and irrevocably his penis sags and shrivels back to the size and consistency of a marshmallow.

James wants to cry.

Serena wants to kill him. Ugh. Why can't he be young? Why doesn't he realise how unattractive he is? He's got access to a mirror like anyone else, hasn't he? He's too old to still be wanting it at his age, he really is. He should have the good grace to give up expecting to have sex with anyone, much less her, and do what she said, take up gardening and bowls or something or just go and die like all old people must.

'Bloody hell! bloody hell! What are you playing at? I can't even brush my teeth in peace now! You've just had it, why don't you admit it! You've had it! You're past it! If you can't do it with me you've got no chance with anyone! The readers of "Turn Me On" magazine, the widest read TV listings publication in the country, have voted me "The Most Attractive Woman In A Soap" for three years running. If you can't do it with me you're done for!'

Miserably Serena goes back to bed. She makes a quick phone call to Mark Turnbull-Ash, the producer of 'Coombe Ridge Crescent'. It's late but he's an insomniac and likes people to ring him in the middle of the night otherwise he starts to feel impossibly alone. They chat about this and that, then Serena happens to ask how the interviews for the part of her long-lost younger sister who's coming back from Australia for the first time in 23 years are going. She's heard, through the grapevine, that Christine Cazale is up for the part and she wonders, does he know, not that it probably makes any difference, he would probably not even consider taking on such an inexperienced actress to play such a vital role, but does he know, actually and in fact, about Christine's chronic recurring problem with cold sores? Then she puts down the phone, wordlessly turns out the light and instantly falls into a deep, angry sleep.

*

James doesn't know what to do. Things with Serena are going from bad to worse to some place so awful only married people know where it is. He feels like shit. His erection is back. He wants to ring Geraldine to see if he can get her to talk him out of it over the phone – Geraldine is sometimes amenable to the odd bit of phone sex – but the last thing she said to him at lunch was not to ring her again until it was to say he'd left his wife. Jesus. His life is so unsatisfactory. He is the most famous actor in the country, he's got a cock the size of Big Ben and here he is, alone, at midnight, frustrated and miserable. Only Shakespeare could understand a man of his tragic stature.

He goes to stand at the bedroom window. How wretched his life is. It simply can't get any worse. He leans out of the window and lets the sharp night air smack him hard in the face. It occurs to him that he could stand on the sill and jump and all his problems would be over. It would be quite a drop, into the basement terrace. He'd be quite dead. He looks down.

Somebody's beaten him to it, for Christ's sake!

There's a body already there. A dead body. Jesus. It's Geraldine. His eyes aren't what they once were but there's no mistaking her dreadful dress sense. What the fuck is Geraldine doing down there? And dead! The stupid cow. She always did take things that one step too far. Yes, she was consumed with love for him, he knew that, but really – to go and kill herself? And in front of his own house? It really was too much. He might have guessed this was how things would end up, with some ridiculously melodramatic act of folly on her part. Now it would be all over the papers, Serena would find out and leave him for his infidelity and he'd be fucked. So to speak.

What's he supposed to do now?

His first instinct is to close the curtains again, go to bed and hope it will all simply go away. He doesn't know how it will but maybe it just will. Things do sometimes work themselves out for the best if you leave them alone and ignore them – that's usually been his tactic with women and it's worked pretty well up till now. When they get obsessional or overwrought or threatening or pregnant – you just disappear and eventually they do too.

Serena looks like she is fast asleep. All James needs to do is remove and relocate the body. Then the problem is no longer his but somebody else's. Geraldine's so bloody thin, she'd be easy to carry. He could move her to the car and then take her somewhere. He wonders where he should go. There's hardly any petrol in the Jag and he's been drinking so a long journey is out. He decides he'll just drive her down to the towpath and leave her there, by the river. It's just the sort of romantic location Geraldine herself would have approved of.

Having defined his plan he starts to feel himself tremble with excitement at the prospect of delivering himself of this horror. He makes a pact with God that if he gets away with this, he will be happier, he will put up with his lot and not complain about anything, not even Serena.

He pulls on a jumper over the T-shirt and a pair of old cords. He creeps down to the kitchen and opens the French doors to the little basement patio. Geraldine has rather inconsiderately fallen right on top of the box tree arrangement that Serena had the landscape gardeners install only last week – she's not going to be pleased about that. (She being Serena not Geraldine of course – Geraldine's past worrying about that kind of thing.)

It's bloody freezing outside. James removes bits of wisteria from his mistress's face – he wonders whether he is doing this out of tenderness or to remove clues. It's the latter, he concedes silently, guiltily to himself.

But then, because he is only human after all, he is suddenly sad – as he thinks of the sex he will no longer be getting and Geraldine's rather lovely penthouse apartment with its jacuzzi bath and vast drinks cabinet which he will no longer be visiting. He even feels a tear at the corner of one eye, dammit.

But needs must and he scoops up his mistress's lifeless form from the basement patio and starts ferrying her over the front lawn. She weighs nothing – and for once he is grateful for all those extended visits to the lavatory she had after every meal when she went to sick up the contents of her stomach in order to stay skinny enough to have a body as voluptuous as a bicycle frame. He is not as fit as he might be and if one's mistress is going to kill herself in front of one's house, it's most obliging of them to be light enough to transport with ease to the car boot afterwards. He gets as far as the car when he remembers he's forgotten to bring out the car keys. He deposits her on the pavement, tenderly he thinks, although her head does take rather a jolt when it hits the ground, and stumbles back through the French doors into the kitchen to retrieve them – only to find, to his horror, Serena who is standing waiting for him in the kitchen.

'Serena! I thought you were asleep,' he squeals.

'What the hell is going on?' she demands, like a good wife does. 'What is all this racket? And what the fuck has happened to my geometric hedge arrangement outside? What are people going to think when they next come to the house for a feature in an interiors lifestyle magazine? It looks like a bomb's dropped out there!'

He is about to lie, about to tell a tale, spin a yarn, anything rather than just tell it like it is. But then he looks at her and thinks – why not, why not just tell the truth? He's too exhausted to do anything else. And maybe if she realised he had a girlfriend it would shock her out of her snotty, superior attitude, make her appreciate the sort of man she was lucky enough to be married to, show her that even if she didn't value him there were other women who did – women prepared to kill themselves for him! Yes. The more he thinks about it, the more he likes this idea.

'Not a bomb actually. A woman.'

'What? What woman?'

'The woman I've been having an affair with for the past year.'

'And you let her make that mess in my garden?'

'Our garden.'

'I found the landscape gardener! I had the concept!' Serena yells. 'And where's this woman now?'

'On the pavement. She's dead.'

It occurs to James at this point that of course a dead girlfriend doesn't have quite the same clout as a live one – it's harder to be jealous of a cadaver.

'Dead?'

'Yes. She was climbing up the front of the house – I had ended the relationship, you see, but she was desperate, so desperate to be with me. Which is, well, I suppose, pretty understandable really. Anyway, she fell and she's dead. So I went down and picked her up and carried her to the car and then I –'

'You did what?'

'Well, I know, it sounds a bit mad. I know that. But I carried her to the front of the house then I came in to get the car keys because I was going to drive her to –'

'You idiot! Why didn't you call the press?'

'The press?'

'The press? The press? Of course the bloody press! Can you imagine the publicity I'd get from that! Wronged wife; cheating husband; dead lover lying in front of the house. It would be perfect, you stupid man! We'd be in the papers for months! I'd be famous forever!'

Serena stands and makes for the phone.

'Are you insane?' he shouts. 'What are you doing?'

'I'm ringing Gareth to get his professional advice as to how we can best maximise the potential of this media opportunity!' she yells back at him. 'You go out there and move her body back to where it was so the whole thing looks more realistic.'

'What do you mean – more realistic? It is really real! She really is dead out there, you silly bitch!'

But Serena isn't listening, she's already dialling Gareth's number. James realises he's going to have to move quickly or Serena's going to destroy them both. He grabs his keys and leaps back outside to get the body, shove it in the car and get it as far away as possible.

But when he gets outside Geraldine is gone anyway.

James looks everywhere for her but Geraldine has definitely left. She was so dead though! For her simply, magically to have disappeared hardly seems possible but it appears that it is – his pact with the Lord seems to have worked. He's worried now about the bit about honouring the part where he'll be happy and won't complain about anything, even Serena. That's going to be difficult, he's just going to have to do his best, he reflects as he goes back into the house.

When he gets into the kitchen Serena is still on the phone.

'He's bloody engaged! How can he be engaged at this time of night? It's that bloody Christine Cazale, I knew he was spending more time on furthering her professional interests than he is on mine!'

James sits down at the table opposite her. 'You can put down the phone,' he says quietly. 'There's no point.'

'Don't you bloody tell me what I can and can't do!' Serena screams.

'I mean it. She's not there. She's gone.'

'You said she was dead!'

'Yes, I thought she was but obviously she wasn't quite dead enough and now she's gone.'

With a look of contempt and disgust Serena runs out to see for herself.

Eventually she comes back into the house. 'How could you be so bloody careless!' she moans. 'You can't even keep your girlfriend dead outside long enough for the press to get here!'

She stands with her hands on her hips in front of him. She says, 'I've decided to leave you, James.'

'Fair enough,' he sighs. He hasn't the energy left for an argument now.

'Just as soon as I've found myself a new permanent boyfriend and Gareth gives it the green light – that'll be the end of us. I may have a break-down or launch my own jewellery line first. We'll have to see how it fits in with my schedule. Then you can pack your stuff and leave.'

'But this is my house. It was my parents' house before me!'

'Don't be ridiculous, James. I'm your wife and I'm going to leave you. Nothing is yours any more.'

CHAPTER 5

It's early morning and all the Xerxes Carmen clothes have just been delivered. Serena would like to stay in all day trying them on but she's got to go and help out at that bloody literacy class Gareth has arranged for her. She's still not at all sure about this voluntary work crap. She rings him. 'Gareth, I'm not at all sure about this voluntary work crap,' she says because she's a woman who likes to say what she thinks. She tells him she just doesn't feel cut out for teaching the unemployed to read and write. Surely there was something else she could do for the down and outs? Something a bit more glamorous – like showing them how to put on fake tan in the difficult bits, or how to choose a really good hairdresser?

Gareth reminds her he's only looking after her best interests and starts ranting on about the fame thing again. Serena immediately feels herself losing interest. And she can see from where she is standing talking on the phone in the drawing room watching herself in the mirror standing talking on the phone in the drawing room that her driver is already on his way up the steps to their front door to collect her. She can hear Evelyn, their maid, going to answer the door. Life goes on around her but no one really understands her. Not Gareth, droning away in her ear, not James pacing out his lines in his study, no one. She has so much to offer! And no one to offer it to! And she is so fucking stunning!

'OK, OK, stop moaning, Gareth. I'll do it. The car's here now, anyway.'

'Good,' says Gareth. 'I'll have the press release ready for the magazines by the time you get back. The photographers are all there waiting for you.'

Serena sighs. She checks her reflection again. She's wearing a navy blue jersey wraparound dress with metallic leather inserts from her new wardrobe of Xerxes Carmen clothes. Gareth said to put on something sensible but sexy. Serena feels the dress answers the brief well. Sensible – it's just about long enough to cover her arse. Sexy – her breasts look like they may escape at any moment. Her long chestnut hair is looped up casually at the back of her head. She's got the Xerxes Carmen brooch fastened discreetly at her waist. She looks at her reflection again. She had considered wearing reading glasses. She thought that would give her a suitable sort of literary look. Then she could take them off and suck on one of the stems while she was being interviewed. People would get the idea. But she hadn't had time to get reading glasses; she wished she'd made the effort now, reading glasses she could take off and suck would have been good. It's too late now. She has no glasses. Shit. It's just too bloody late now.

Is she going to be able to cope with the disappointment?

Evelyn taps respectfully at the door and reminds her that the car is waiting. Serena checks her lips, lashes and armpits and goes to the door. It's too bad about the glasses but somehow she's just going to have to pull through.

She checks her reflection again on the way out in the hall mirror. Maybe that cleavage is a bit too risky – she wouldn't want to come across as tarty. She unpins the Xerxes Carmen brooch from her waist and moves it up to her chest to give the fabric of the dress at least a fighting chance of holding itself together for the duration of the morning. She sees her driver looking at his watch. One last pout in the mirror then Serena Dawlish sweeps out to go and improve her caring profile.

*

When Serena arrives at the literacy centre a small posse of local dignitaries, social workers, photographers and members of the public who'll go anywhere where there's a crowd are waiting for her. As the driver opens her door there is a spontaneous ripple of applause. This is a woman they see almost every evening on the telly. This is Susan Depton. This is

Serena Dawlish. She's like magic. Different, better than them. Cameras flash. Serena opens her legs wide as she gets out of the back of the BMW, stretching the skirt of the wraparound dress to the very limits of its endurance. Cameras flash harder.

A middle-aged man shuffles forward.

'Miss Dawlish, I'd like to take this opportunity at this time to introduce myself – I'm Mr David, well, Dave, Carter, Head of the Reading and Writing Group. I'd like to say how I'm so thrilled to have you.'

You can only dream about having me, Serena thinks wearily as she watches the sweat erupt and cascade on his forehead. Couldn't they have found someone younger and better-looking to have greeted her? What's he going to look like in the photos? Bloody awful, that's what.

A small girl with buck teeth presents her with a bouquet of flowers in colours that clash with her dress. She's not sure she's going to be able to take any more of this. She wants to ring Gareth and tell him she just can't do it. Other stars throw tantrums, why can't she? Why isn't Gareth here anyway, the arsehole?

A man grabs her shoulder. She swings round, ready to give him mouthful, when she sees the TV camera behind him.

'A few words for the "Real Live Celebrities" show?' the man asks.

'Oh sure!' Serena exclaims. Finally! Air she can breathe!

'This is pretty splendid, coming down to your local literacy centre and giving some of your time to those less fortunate than yourself.'

'Well, of course being an actress I'm passionate about the arts, about the spoken word, so I thought it made sense to help those who aren't bright enough to even have been able to learn to read properly.'

'Is it true that Christine Cazale is being considered for the part of your long-lost sister?'

'Christine who?'

'And is it true that Rod Swathey, the actor who plays your current husband Gary in "Coombe Ridge Crescent" is threatening to leave the series because of . . . a character clash with you?'

'A character clash? Is that what he's calling it? Well, I'm not surprised, I know that in recent weeks, what with his wife being pregnant and having put on all that weight, I think working so closely with me has become very . . . challenging for him.'

'So are you telling us that romance blossomed on set?'

'Look, I'm sorry. I really can't get into that now, I'm here to help others less fortunate than myself, to do what I can to help the illiterate and the ignorant make something of their sad, empty lives and the problems in Rod's marriage just aren't that high on my agenda right now. I wish him well, I really do, and I hope that one day the wounds of rejection will heal for him, that's all I can say at this time, OK?'

Other interviewers fight their way to the front, more questions are asked, banalities exchanged, but with lips and tits like hers it isn't really the dialogue that matters. Eventually Dave Carter intervenes, manfully extracts her from the journalists and takes her down an orange corridor to a green room full of blue plastic chairs and yellow plastic tables where a motley selection of suitably low-achieving adults are standing in line waiting for her.

'These are the literacy students here,' Dave Carter trills proudly as if presenting a row of prize marrows. Serena stands and stares. 'You might want to go and shake them all by the hand,' Dave whispers into her ear. 'I think it's what they're expecting.' Serena ignores him. She only does body contact when she's being paid for it and even then only when Gareth has made sure the right caveats have been written into the contract.

'What happens now?' Serena asks irritably. 'Do I pick one of them?'

Dave Carter is still standing obnoxiously close to her, breathing heavily. His clammy hand is gripping her elbow and from the state of his trousers it is clear he'd be happy to be sharing another part of his anatomy with her as well. 'Not yet, no, Miss Dawlish. When we're ready, I'm sure we can find you a suitable student to work with. Obviously it would be best if you link up with the same person every week. Then you can get to know them and they can get to know . . . you.' Dave Carter looks for all the world as if he wished he was suddenly bereft of literacy so he could be that one. 'Obviously,' he adds, 'they'd all give their left arm to be taught to read and write by the famous Serena Dawlish!'

'Every week? I don't think so! I've come here today, Mr Carter, and already sacrificed an entire morning. You can hardly expect me to come back next week!'

'But teaching someone to read and write . . .'

'Yes! Of course! Well I'm here this morning – there's a lot you can learn in a morning isn't there? I'll read a bit and I'll write a bit and then my job will be done, won't it?'

The students in the selection line shuffle nervously, hoping against hope to be chosen. They have their autograph books ready. Some are taking photos of her with their mobile phones.

This is not going well but Dave Carter is not sure how to make it go any better. Serena scans the assembled gathering of people up and down, her heart sinking. They all look common. They all look as if they need to change their underwear more often. She wants to turn and run. She's done the interview, they've taken the photos. Why doesn't she turn and run?

Then she sees him.

Sitting at the far end of the room, scribbling in a notebook, there is a tall fair-haired man with a body she knows, even from a distance, even with him sitting down, she wants to be underneath. This is a man who could satisfy her, she's sure of that, don't ask her how, she just is.

'Who's that?' she demands.

'Who? Him over there? That's Marlon, Marlon Drayton. I'm sorry, he refused to stand up. He's new, he's very difficult, I knew it would upset you, Miss Dawlish, but you have to understand, we can't force –'

'I want to talk to him,' she lies, because talking is the last thing on her mind.

'I don't think –' Dave Carter begins but his words are lost – she's gone. She heads off towards the man's table and when she gets there sits down opposite him.

'Hi,' she says simply, because that's usually all it takes. He looks up. She waits for him to have a violent physical reaction, a spontaneous irresistible craving for her. He doesn't. He looks back at his notebook and starts scribbling more numbers.

'What are you doing?' she asks sweetly.

'Calculating the relationship of prime numbers against the anagramic biorhythm of a star.'

'Oh, that's nice,' she says. 'Is that what you do, then, is it, sort of maths and stuff?'

'Yes.'

'Yes, I love maths too. I got a C for my maths GCSE. They told me I'd fail but I showed them!'

The man appears unimpressed. God, he is so fucking handsome!

'Do you not realise who I am?' she asks, pouting, her lips very slightly parted.

He looks at her again, this time with irritation. He puts down his pencil and sighs.

He shakes his head.

Serena gives a tinkly little laugh. 'Are you sure?' she simpers.

Marlon stares at her for a few moments. He examines her face carefully then looks her body up and down. He studies her cleavage. Suddenly he goes pale.

'Oh no!' he cries. He stands and backs away from her. 'Oh no!' he cries again. 'It can't be!'

'Yes! It can! It is!' she giggles excitedly.

Marlon is staggering, clutching onto the chair, the wall, the blood is burning in his temples. He has seen her chest. He has realised who she is.

She is one of them.

She is an alien

Dave Carter intervenes. 'Miss Dawlish, may I just say – perhaps it's best not to start with this young man. It's only his first day and –'

'I like this one. This is the one I want,' Serena insists, pointing a perfect purple nail in Marlon's direction. 'Isn't there a room where he and I can work privately?' she asks.

David Carter is now a deeply unhappy man. He has spent weeks planning The Day's Schedule for Serena's visit and this kind of an incident didn't feature on it anywhere. 'Well, no, I'm sorry, Miss Dawlish, it's not as simple as that. It's not just a question of finding a room. The point is, you haven't even had your training yet! I was going to personally show you my –'

'Training? How long will that take?'

'Well, about once a week for 5 weeks . . .'

'Don't be ridiculous! I can't wait that long!' Serena squeals.

Meanwhile they both realise that something is wrong with Marlon. Still ogling Serena's bust, he appears to be having some sort of fit. He is standing, trembling, his eyes pulsating in their sockets. Dave Carter looks across at him, appalled. 'Oh, don't worry,' Serena waves it away with her hand. 'This is what I do to men. It'll pass. I'll sort him out.'

But it is soon clear that whatever is going on with Marlon is not something that is going to go away easily. He is consumed with a violent shaking, his face goes blue. His hand reaches up and points to her breasts. 'Look! Look!' he cries. 'Look there!'

Yeh, yeh, tell me something I don't know, Serena thinks wearily. Most of the men in the room have been looking there ever since she arrived.

'I'm so sorry, Miss Dawlish,' Dave Carter begins. 'I'll ask for someone to –'

'The sign!' Marlon wails, indicating her brooch. 'The XC sign!' For the past ten years Marlon has known the aliens were on their way to earth. He knew he would be able to chart their movements by plotting the trajectories of the stars against prime numbers. XC is the mathematical formula he has discovered which connects the prime numbers with the stars (XC being, of course, the simpler expression of $\bar{a} = Li + (x) \Omega\, 3s - 2/6 = (\lambda)\, \Delta$). It seems the moment of truth is here. They have finally landed and she is one of them. Although his first instinct is to run away in terror he summons up his courage and forces himself to be brave, to remember his strategy – to ally and infiltrate then vanquish. He is ready for them, they will not be a match for him. He stands and addresses her.

'I know who you are,' he states with as firm a voice as he can muster.

Serena nods. 'I think you'll find most people do,' she laughs.

'I am Marlon Drayton,' he announces, enunciating each word slowly and methodically as one does when talking to someone from another planet. 'I am a human man. You must teach me what you know. I will teach you what I know. I will come with you.'

As chat-up lines go, Serena has heard better. But then she's heard worse too.

'Come on then, sweetheart,' she says brushing the bewildered Mr Carter aside and taking her human man firmly by the hand.

*

Serena and Marlon are smooching in the back of her BMW on the way back from the Literacy Centre. At this stage of a relationship Serena would normally be having full intercourse but that's OK – she can still appreciate the novelty of a guy who likes to take his time. And Marlon, she can tell, is a shy boy. He's very responsive but she has to do everything first. She kisses him – he kisses her back. She puts her tongue in his mouth – he puts his tongue in hers. She puts his hand on her breast – he gropes her. He's very good at all of it, she's got no complaints, but he does need a lot of help getting started and when it comes to penetration – well, he's going to have to take the lead on that, isn't he?

Marlon is trying to keep up with the alien woman's physical examination of him which is very vigorous and intense. Although he was able to identify her as an alien, she has been so well constructed that there are in fact only a few tell-tale signs that she is extraterrestrial. The wide, almost popping eyes; the unnaturally even little nose; the bright white impossibly straight teeth; the strangely narrow hips and staggeringly large breasts. These minor aberrations aside, he cannot get over how this alien woman has managed to morph herself into something so close to human form. Her message to him is clear – she wants him to know how good that form is. She is inviting him to inspect all her parts – the inside of her mouth, the contours of her chest, even the structure up between her legs. She is anatomically near faultless. How many humans have they taken and dissected in their laboratories to be able to study the physiognomy so well? They must have made more progress than he had anticipated. What is even more disconcerting is that if she is so willing to offer her body for inspection it must mean that she does not care if he knows she is extraterrestrial. Why is that? Is his life already as good as over? They have identified him as their next specimen, as their next subject for experiment, that much is clear, but what are they trying to tell him now? Is their plan to lure him in, win him over, then use him in some foul way?

What should he do?

Serena's driver, meanwhile, is patiently going round in tight elliptical circles up and down Brentford High Street tactfully waiting for instructions while Serena makes up her mind whether to risk taking Marlon back to hers or not. Eventually lust overcomes her and she instructs the driver to go to the house but when they arrive her husband is standing talking on the phone at the bedroom window and she realises this is madness.

She explains the situation to Marlon, that this is her house but now is not the right time. 'Shall we go back to your place?' she says with a cute smile. She's not averse to doing it in the back of a car but for a first date she's enough of a romantic to wait for a bed.

'OK,' Marlon mutters. She's obviously changed her mind, for some extraterrestrial reason only she knows, not to let him see her headquarters just yet. But perhaps it is for the best. If he is going to be dissected maybe he would rather have it done in the comfort of his own home.

She tells him to give the driver his address. He knows they must already know exactly where he lives but obviously they work to different data than street names. He accepts that this alien wants to enter his home so she can observe his habitat. But as soon as he's given the address he starts to feel anxious and sick. He's just not ready for her just yet. He can't explain it – he knew it was going to happen, of course he did, but now that it has, it's all happened so quickly and he doesn't feel strong enough, he doesn't feel brave enough to cope. He's not ready, he's not. But what can he do? If he shows reluctance, if he hesitates he may lose her trust. If he does not show her his place she may not show him hers. And he has to see where they operate, for it is only when he has understood more about their set-up that he can work out how he, single-handedly, is going to foil them.

The car sets off. Her house is only a moment away from Marlon's flat, across the Half Acre. This does not surprise him: of course she was going to find a base close to his, all the better to observe him from. He begins to tremble with doubt and trepidation. He must conquer his fear, he tells himself. He won't be able to think straight if he doesn't relax.

Serena is ecstatic. What a morning's work! Caring profile in the bag, plus she's hooked herself this gorgeous hunk into the bargain. Ooh, he's lovely. And she's got him going all right. He took a while to get started but now he can't take his eyes off her, he's staring at her, literally staring, and he's lying back in the seat with his legs wide open, doing this kind of heavy breathing thing, and he's shivering with longing for her. She can see his big strong muscles bulging through his shirt. Better still she can feel his lovely big erection forcing its way out of his trousers. Finally – a proper man. As she fondles it she giggles and says, 'I hope you're going to let me examine this in closer detail when we get back to yours.'

'This is the part you're particularly interested in, is it?' he asks.

She laughs. He's weird but gorgeous.

'Oh yes,' she says giving it an enthusiastic squeeze. 'I'm sure I'm going to be getting to know this bit of you very well.'

'I understand – who you are,' he splutters.

Serena sighs. 'Oh yes, I know that. But really, don't let it put you off. I mean you know, I'm just like anyone else really. Well, yes, I know, that's not strictly true –'

'No –'

'But I do try to lead as normal a life as possible.' She sighs again. 'To be honest it's hard going out and doing every day things like shopping and clubbing because, you know, I don't want people to see me and start pointing and making a fuss.'

'No, of course not. I can understand that.'

He never expected this kind of candour. He finds it strangely endearing. But then he chides himself and puts himself back on his guard. This might be all part of her plan, to put him at his ease so she can lure him deeper in.

'Anyway, we don't need to worry about any of that do we?

Soon it'll be just you and me and then we can really show each other what we're made of!'

'We will show each other? So – you don't expect me to do everything? You will also participate?'

'Participate! Bloody hell darling, this is the twenty-first century! Girls like me, we do more than participate! When I'm done with you you'll have to lie down for a week to recover!'

This seems to frighten him. Blimey, he's a bit of a wimp, Serena thinks to herself. 'Only kidding!' she giggles. Then whispers conspiratorially in his ear, 'It might only be a few days, not a whole week.'

I must be brave, I must be strong, Marlon reminds himself.

When they get to the place where Marlon lives Serena is unimpressed. She doesn't know what she was expecting but she wasn't expecting this – a bloody council estate. Serena's from a detached home with period style conservatory and double garage in Gerrards Cross – she's not programmed to cope with council estates. Anyway she just can't afford to be seen going into a place like this. The people who live in places like this are the sort of people who watch her on TV. On TV she's the sort of person who lives in a place like this. So they don't want to see her here in real life. No. In real life they want to see her in the top hotels and fashionable bars decorated in neon and zinc and restaurants with leather tables and fluffy wallpaper. Otherwise they're just not going to believe in her, are they?, they're just not going to take her seriously when she pretends to be a poor single mother on the TV four times a week. They don't want her to actually be one of them, do they?, otherwise it wouldn't be acting, it would just be like a bloody boring documentary or something and no one wants to watch one of those.

She's desperate to get her teeth into this hunk – but what can she do? They can't do it here, James is at home and a hotel's not an option, she daren't risk be photographed going to a hotel for sex with a man who is not a celebrity.

When they get to his flat Marlon can see immediately – to his immense relief – that all she wanted to do today was confirm his location. Whatever else she has planned for him, it is not going to happen now.

'Look,' she says, 'I would come up now but the thing is I'm working to a bit of a schedule today.'

Marlon nods. 'Every day you have things you must do, things you must achieve, you are working to a plan, a plan set by others.'

'Yes, yes, that's it.' God, she wishes her husband was as understanding as this. 'But I want to see you later. This afternoon. OK?'

'Yes, OK,' Marlon replies stoically.

Hadn't James told her he was out later for a rehearsal? She was sure he had. 'Later you can come back to my place. We can do it there.'

'It?'

'You know,' she drools, 'that examination of your gorgeous body I've got lined up for you.'

'Will we be alone?'

'Oh yes, quite alone, don't worry about that.'

'You don't mind me seeing your . . . place?'

'No! Course not. Obviously I'm normally very private but I'm making an exception for you, darling. Anyway, we need privacy for what we're going to be doing. I might need you to sign a little contract first to say you're not going to go public on anything, that's OK with you, isn't it?'

Marlon's knees have started knocking. He just can't help himself. 'Look,' he stammers, 'I need to ask you . . . what are you going to do to me?'

'Ha! Do you think I'm going to tell you that now?! You shall just have to wait and see what I've got planned for you, boy!'

'And if I choose not to do what you ask, not to obey?'

This is more like it! Forget James and his baggy T-shirt and his droopy dick – this is the kind of relationship she wants – a handsome young man who can give her a bit of edge, a bit of excitement.

'Disobey me? I don't think so. You could try of course. But I may get angry. I may get very, very angry. Then I shall have to tie you up and whip you!'

'I understand,' Marlon replies coldly. Their brutality did not surprise him; their openness did. He had imagined them more manipulative. There was no subterfuge – they laid their plans out frankly. Perhaps he should respond in kind.

'And if I show you how I work, will you show me how you are constructed?'

'Oh yes, darling, I'll certainly do that!'

'And will you tell me what your intentions are?'

'Bad, all bad!' she squeals. 'Look, it's 11 now. I'll send my driver round to get you at 3. Is that OK?'

Maybe she needs to go back to set up her laboratory first, Marlon thinks.

'Here,' she says, 'before you go, you can't keep your eyes off my chest can you? Why don't you take this brooch and keep it as a memento.' Gareth can always get Xerxes Carmen to send round another one. She unpins it from her dress and hands it to him. 'Feel it – it's still warm from my skin.' He takes the brooch.

'This is your . . . sign.'

'Well, if you like. Let's just say it's my little gift to you. I give you that little thing now – you give me something big later! Is that a deal?' she sniggers.

Marlon's hands begin to shake as he holds the brooch. XC. He has been right all along.

He turns, terrified, to get out of the car. He's got a lovely bum. She says, 'You're perfect, do you know that? You're the perfect specimen.'

'Right,' he mumbles, shaking.

'I want your body, Marlon, I really do,' she calls after him.

'I want your heart, your soul, your mind, I want everything, I want it all. And this afternoon, I'm going to get it. This afternoon it'll be s-e-x all the way.'

He looks at her blankly.

'Oh, sorry, love, I forgot – s-e-x spells sex,' she clarifies.

Marlon leaves the car and walks slowly up to the flat. He is terrified. She doesn't care at all that he knows who she is. What can he do? He has to get close enough to this creature to be able to find out her plans. He thinks he is clever enough to stay one step ahead of her but what if he is not and she annihilates him before he can stop her and all her fellow aliens taking over?

For years now he has done the maths and studied the stars through his telescopes. He knows that the answer to everything lies in the relationship between the stars and prime numbers. He has all the best equipment. Lightbridges, astrofinders, refractor filters, deep sky imagers, spotting scopes, pirate scopes – his mother reads out all the descriptions in the catalogues to him and he tells her what to order, what he needs. Then the information is all there, in the numbers and in the night sky. The quasars and pulsars speak to him, the comets and the novae give him messages only he can translate. It is all there, on display, there for anyone to see and comprehend, it's just that he's the only one who can. Only his mathematical genius and his knowledge of the stars can save mankind. He has made his calculations, interpreted his equations, filled hundreds of notebooks full of formulae recording what he has observed. That's how he knew the aliens were coming.

He feels the weight of his responsibility heavy on his broad shoulders. He has a mission, a duty. A destiny. Because they are here, they are here and they will not rest until Earth is theirs.

He's doing all this for his mum. To save her. How can he tell her how much he loves her? He cannot. He could not even begin. But when he, he alone, saves the planet, and everyone in it, everyone including her, then she will understand. Then she will be so happy, so grateful. Then, then she will realise the extent of his love for her, his mother. And all those people on the estate, those people who shout stuff through the letterbox and call him a sad loser, a poofter, 26 and still living at home, and laugh at him, yes! Yes! They will not be laughing then. Not laughing when they realise it is he, Marlon Drayton, who has saved the world from the invaders. And all those people who call his mum a fat slag, they will be worshipping her then. Yes, they will. They will recognise her as the mother of the man who saved the world. They won't be laughing then.

CHAPTER 6

Shelley is sitting at her kitchen table eating prawn and onion crisps and a hot sausage and bacon sandwich. She is writing a letter. It's a very personal letter about her life. It doesn't make for an easy read, that much is sure. It's a letter which is full of passion, pain and pathos. It's a letter which only someone with the hardest heart could read without feeling the salt-water tears welling at their eyes.

It describes how Shelley was abandoned at a bus stop by her mother as a baby (cardboard box, no note) and brought up in a home where she was forced to sleep on a stone floor and beaten regularly by one of the matrons in the home who was jealous of Shelley's golden hair. How she fought an addiction to drugs and alcohol in her teens. How she lost the use of both legs in a terrible accident at the factory where she worked and now struggles to bring up her 5 kids single-handedly. How each of the fathers of the children promised her on their mother's life that they would stay with her and that's the only reason she had sex with them because of her craving for love and affection which is understandable really, she's only a woman after all.

It could happen to anyone. There but for the grace of God go you.

At this point the microwave pings. Shelley gets up to take out her chicken and ham pie and make a cup of tea, then she goes back to her writing. This letter, she's got to be honest, is not as good as yesterday's. She was feeling much more artistic with her words yesterday. In yesterday's letter she'd lived with her parents until she was 9 then they were both killed in a plane crash flying back from a holiday in Torremolinos, a holiday where they had gone just the two of them for a romantic reunion after being separated for six months after an argument over a vacuum cleaner. The young Shelley had been so thrilled to have her mum and dad back together – only to have all her dream smashed in that plane accident. When that plane crashed so did all her hope of happiness. She had then – understandably – gone on to fight an addiction to drugs and alcohol in her teens, brought up 5 kids etc etc.

She always does a letter every morning. One classified ad in the paper every Sunday – 'Pennyless singel mum at witts end, please help' – is all it takes. She gets offers from all over the country, even from overseas. Sometimes they just send cash straight to the post office box number, usually they want a letter telling them a bit more about how bad things are for her so they can feel even better about themselves when they send her the money.

Of course she could just send the same letter out every time but that would be ripping people off, wouldn't it?, simply churning out the same story without putting in any effort. That's just not the sort of woman Shelley is.

And it doesn't matter that none of it is strictly true. The fact is she needs this money. Not for herself, for her son, Marlon. She needs it to pay for his equipment. She's got a job, writing the poems for the insides of greetings cards. She works hard at that but it only pays for the food and the bills, it doesn't earn her anywhere like enough what her Marlon needs for all his telescopes and stuff. So she has to write the letters – what else can she do?

Suddenly she looks at the clock and panics – she's let herself get carried away and not noticed it's 11 am, time for the repeat of the repeat of 'Coombe Ridge Crescent'. They show the new episode every weekday afternoon, then the repeat of that late the same evening, then the second repeat the following morning. As far as Shelley's concerned it gets better with each showing. She always watches the first showing of each episode down on the big flat screen in the pub, then the next two at home on her battered telly in the kitchen. She can hardly wait to watch it again – the bit where Sue discovers that her best friend, Jenny, has just spent the night with her ex-boyfriend.

'But, Sue!' wails this Jenny slag, 'you told me it was all over between you and Nigel!'

'Don't give me that!' Sue cries back, 'it may have all been over and I may be married to Gary now but that doesn't mean I don't still have feelings for Nigel! That doesn't give you the right to sleep with him!'

Shelley finishes the letter off a bit sharpish, scribbling down something about how without their help she's not quite sure how she's going to be able to carry on and she may have to end it all, then she puts a few stains from her tea on the edge of the paper, folds it up, shoves it in an envelope then flicks on the remote.

Just then Marlon comes in. He's her only child and she would fight to the death for him and it doesn't even matter to her that he's as odd as he is but why can't he learn not to interrupt her when 'Coombe Ridge' is on?

'Do you know what time it is?' she snaps at him.

'I keep sidereal time, mum, you know that.'

'It's 11, the repeat of "Coombe Ridge Crescent" is gonna start any minute!'

'That crap,' he mumbles as he extracts a three cheese and pepperoni pizza from the icy bowels of the fridge freezer and starts fiddling with the knobs on the oven.

'Can't you just shove it in the microwave so it's done before "Coombe Ridge" starts?'

He looks at her with horror. 'You must be joking. I'd be a walking transmitter if I did. Full of ELF rays. You do realise that microwave radiation can alter the synapses of the brain?' he says.

Not all this again, she thinks. It's such a pity. He's so tall, so fit, so gorgeous, there's nothing about him that isn't perfect. Apart from what's inside his head.

'Yes, love, I think you mentioned that to me before,' she mumbles. She doesn't give a toss what a synapse is, and she doesn't care – just as long as he's out of her way before her programme starts.

'Does it never occur to you,' he asks, 'that the first microwave was invented sometime around 1946? And that the Roswell crash took place in July of 1947? What does that tell you?'

It tells me you're beautiful but weird, Shelley thinks.

'I don't know, love. You know I'm not really one for all that historical stuff. I've enough problems coping with the present. I tell you what,' she says impatiently because time is running out, 'you go back in the lounge to play, I mean work, with your telescopes and I'll sort out your snack and call you when it's ready, only let me watch my programme in peace.'

'You should let me do it,' he grumbles. 'You should let me do what I want. I'm 26 and you treat me as if I was 6,' he moans but anyway grunts and leaves.

Quickly Shelley shoves everything in the oven then settles down to watch 'Coombe Ridge Crescent'. Within moments Serena Dawlish comes on the screen. As soon as she sees the glamorous, man-eating Sue Upton, that's when Shelley starts to feel the shivers running up and down her spine.

Shelley used to think that she would like to be Sue. Then at some point, things spilled over and she was, she became Sue. She can't do any of that stuff in her real life – not when you're 18 stone you can't – but Sue does it all for her instead, has the affairs, throws the big strops, ends the relationships then starts them again. Three times a day five days a week Shelley is Sue who is Serena. They are all the same.

'Yeah, you tell her, girl,' Shelley yells at the television screen through a mouth full of chicken and ham pie and salt and vinegar crisp. 'You fucking tell her what's what!' she squeals with excitement.

After ten minutes the oven pings and Marlon reappears and

Shelley has to get up and take the pizza out and cut the crust off – Marlon can't abide crusts – which means she misses the bit where Sue confronts Nigel about Jenny. Marlon usually eats in the lounge where all his equipment is but today, for some reason, he sits down with her at the kitchen table. Now it's not that Shelley doesn't love her boy but when 'Coombe Ridge' is on she's just not in the mood for small talk. Anyway then the ads come on so she puts the sound on mute and she makes an effort, just to be nice. And she wants to ask him about the Literacy Class he's just been to. It was his idea to go there, it doesn't make any difference to her whether he can read and write – maths is his thing and we can't be good at everything – but he made up his mind he wanted to go and there was no stopping him. And now that she looks at him properly, he looks a bit, well, peculiar. Maybe they weren't nice to him there, maybe someone took the piss that he's 26 and he still can't read.

'How did that reading class go then?' she says. 'You don't have to go back to it if you don't want to, you know. Are you sure you want to go to it, love? There's no need really, is there? I mean, you've got this far with just your numbers, why bother now with all this reading and writing stuff?'

'I've told you. I have to learn to read. I have to be able to read all their communications to me and they might start using words. They know humans use words so it's the next logical step,' Marlon argues quietly but firmly.

'And they are –?'

'You know who they are.'

'Right. The aliens,' says Shelley. She flops back down in the kitchen chair. What's she going to do about him? Only the one son and he's turned out barmy. Beautiful but barmy. Was it something she had done? Too many chips and fizzy drinks when he was a kid? He'd had an apple every Sunday – had that not been enough?

'Coombe Ridge Crescent' is about to start again. She

reaches for the remote to turn the sound back up but he stops her.

'Listen mum,' he says gravely, 'there's something I've got to tell you. Something important.'

Here we go, Shelley thinks to herself. He's going to come out. She knew it was just a question of time before he announced he was gay. Twenty six, no girlfriend, still living at home with his mum but what can she do? Is it her fault if her boy loves her so much? Here we go. He's going to come out. She braces herself. 'Go on then, Marl,' she says. 'I'm listening, and I want you to know that whatever it is, I'm here for you, love.'

'They're here. They have arrived.'

Oh dear. Not this, please no, don't make it this. Couldn't he just be gay like everyone else? She really wouldn't mind that at all, she's got no problem with gay people. Only last month she completed a new series of cards on a 'Glad To Be Gay' theme, e.g. 'You've Come Out – Congratulations!'; 'You've Told Your Parents – The Worst Is Over!'; 'Happy Civil Partnership Day From Us All!' Gay would be fine, anything would be better than this.

'They've arrived?'

'Yes,' Marlon confirms solemnly. 'The aliens are here. They've actually landed and they, well one of them anyway, has tracked me down and made contact with me. It must have been the microwave. I told you to get rid of it, I told you not to use it but I know you do. But don't worry, I'm not trying to blame you. Sooner or later they were going to catch up with me. Sooner or later they were going to find me.'

Shelley sighs. 'How do you know, Marlon, love? How do you know they've found you?' Shelley asks wearily.

'I told you! Because they've made contact with me. Today, when I was at that reading thing. One of them came and sought me out. She brought me home. She said she's going to come back later and get me. She's going to take me back to her laboratory. And that's going to be it, Mum. She said she can't wait to get her hands on me,' he whispers.

I bet she can't, the tart, Shelley thinks to herself. My gorgeous boy, my precious son. Any woman would want to get her hands on you.

'Marlon, love,' Shelley begins tenderly, not quite knowing what to say. 'This stuff about aliens, you know, all this stuff you believe in, this stuff you've just told me now, about this woman, coming to get you –'

'You don't believe me, do you?' he says miserably. 'Look at this. She gave me this. She was wearing this brooch on the front of her dress and she unpinned it and gave it to me.' He hands her the brooch he has been clutching.

'That's nice dear,' Shelley remarks, her eyes straining up towards the silent TV screen to try and at least catch the bit where Nigel and Sue make it up on the hall carpet. Shelley hasn't had it in years and the way she sees it a bit of passion on 'Coombe Ridge' is the closest she's ever likely to get it again.

'Don't you see! XC is the equation which links prime numbers to the trajectories of the stars I've been charting!'

'Oh, good.' That Nigel, he doesn't leave much to the imagination. Look where he's got his hands!

'But the thing is,' Marlon continues miserably, 'I don't understand why they didn't warn me. I mean, I knew they were coming but I didn't realise it would be now. I didn't realise it would be so soon. I was expecting a sign but there was nothing,' he whines.

Suddenly the television makes a pop sound and the screen dissolves into a million black and white flickers.

'Fuck!' Shelley yells. She goes over to kick the television.

Marlon goes pale. 'Do you think it's a sign they're trying to communicate with me?'

'No, Marlon, love,' his mother replies pragmatically, 'I think it's a sign we need a new telly.'

'But how often do I watch television? Never! And this one

time I've come to sit with you, to tell you about the alien and the brooch, the one time I do, look what happens.'

'Yeah,' says Shelley miserably as she kicks the television again.

'Stop! Stop!' Marlon shouts.

'No, I won't,' she says. 'It's the only way I'm gonna get the bugger working again so I can see the last bit where Nigel and –'

'Look! Look!' he interrupts her. 'Can you see the patterns changing?'

Shelley moves her face closer to the screen and squints.

'No.'

'Yes! Yes! Look! Here!' He traces an outline with his finger on the screen.

She squeezes her eyes as hard as she can. She follows the line of his finger and, now that he mentions it, she can see something, kind of like the shape of a semi-circle with an 'X' cutting across it. It lasts for about twenty seconds during which time Marlon gesticulates furiously and pants loudly with excitement. Eventually the image fades and the screen returns to a random blur.

He holds up the brooch victoriously. 'Look, mum,' he yells, 'Look! It's the brooch, the brooch! How can that be coincidence, Mum? How can it? It's the XC of my mathematical formulae, the things I've been studying all these years! It's no coincidence. It's a communication from them. They are here. They are here!' he cries.

He's right. It was the same sign. It was an XC clear as anything in the flickers on the broken TV screen, identical to the shape of the brooch.

Shelley groans and holds her head in her hands. The only thing worse than a loopy son who thinks the aliens is coming is a loopy son who thinks the aliens are here and might be right.

★

James is in a strange mood. He can't make up his mind

whether to leave his wife or not. Yes, she's said she's going to leave him but he there's no point taking her seriously, women are always making silly threats to get attention. Yes, he was going to dump Geraldine but he's been thinking about her and how yesterday, in his club, she said she wanted him to leave his wife for her and then she was prepared to die, well, almost die to prove her love for him. He had no idea she felt that strongly about him – it's understandable that she does, of course, but still something he had underestimated. The fact is that Geraldine's probably going to make stacks of money from that TV show and that needs to be worked into the equation. One has to be sensible about things, after all. And he's so bloody bored with Serena, so sick of her silly voice and the repulsive smell of her fake tan, and even though he's not exactly in love with Geraldine either, to be honest he's not even sure he likes her that much, she does give a great blow job and that has to count for something.

He's been trying to ring Geraldine up and invite her round for sex and a frank chat about their future but there's been no reply all morning. He thought he'd have the house to himself all day as Serena left early to go to some charity event but she was only out for a couple of hours then came home in a foul mood and went straight to bed. He keeps praying she'll go out again and buy a dress or a new bit of face or whatever it is she goes and spends money on all the time but she's up there in bed, the lazy cow, reading her ghastly celebrity magazines and putting on make-up to try and appear more attractive to him. If only she knew. He can't stand the sight of her at the best of times and when she's all done up like a maypole it's even worse.

All day he keeps giving her hopeful looks that she'll suddenly magically announce she's going out but she doesn't budge. She keeps asking him whether he's got a rehearsal – he has explained that he hasn't, that he is at home to learn his lines but she still keeps asking. She must be panicking he's going to go out and leave her on her own. She obviously wants him to make love to her again but he just can't face all that again, not with her. Really, she is driving him mad.

The fact is, James tells himself, the fact is that he wants Geraldine just as much as she wants him. Yes, he does. He always thought she was only in it for the sex, the dinners, the kudos of being seen with him. But now he knows she really wants him for himself as a man rather than simply as a performer, a name, a star, that she wants him enough to try and kill herself for him – well, the fact is that he can confess he has been aching for this kind of love all his life and he wants her, yes he does, he wants her every bit as much as she wants him.

The afternoon passes, evening comes, Geraldine still isn't replying to any of his calls or texts. James suddenly makes up his mind: he is going to leave Serena, yes, he will leave her and divorce her and marry Geraldine. Suddenly everything is crystal clear in his mind; his destiny unfolds seamlessly before him. He'll be the most famous name in British theatre and she in television and together they will be the golden couple of the performing arts and everything will be perfectly perfect. Marvellous Geraldine. She's so right for him. And so wise to push him to a decision – that kick up the pants was just what he needed.

That's it – he's made his choice now. He can't bear even one more night in the same bed as Serena. He rings up Geraldine and leaves yet another message on her phone. He declares his love to her and says he is going to leave Serena and when would be a good time for him to arrange to have his things sent round to her flat? He's suddenly so excited about having made this decision that he makes another – he's going to go out to the local petrol station to buy Geraldine a card to express his feelings. Women love feelings. He'll send it to her in the morning. That should do the trick.

It is 10 o'clock. He decides he is going to tell Serena that they are out of milk and that he is going to nip down to the garage as he's desperate for a coffee. After that he'll be in his study going over his lines deep into the night and will probably sleep on the divan in there so he doesn't disturb her

He has his story all worked out but when he goes back up to the bedroom to tell her the light is off and she is fast asleep. Poor girl. She has waited all day for him to come up to the bedroom and be with her. It must be so hard for her to be married to a man like him and to know he no longer desires her. For a moment he feels almost sorry for her then he catches a whiff of her fake tan and the sympathy subsides.

*

Serena has been waiting all day for James to go out so she can send her driver round to collect Marlon and bring him to her. When Serena gets nervous she applies extra layers of make-up and by now the surface of her face is buried in foundation and her eyelids can no longer close properly with the amount of sheer shine faux matt eye shadow she has put on them.

Not only has James not gone out but he's been hanging round her all afternoon with a stupid expression on his face like he wants something from her. He must be bloody joking. Every time she sees one of his gormless "how-about-it-darling?" looks she gives him a "no-fucking-way" look back to let him know what his chances are with her.

She's still in bed, sitting up reading 'Watch This'. She's not on the cover of it so she should be pissed off but she's not. She doesn't care. She's been on the same page for the past thirty minutes, staring at nothing, thinking about Marlon. Even though the readers of 'Hot!' magazine voted her best finger-nails in Britain she's chewing at them with nerves; that's the sort of state she's in.

All Serena can think about is Marlon and how bloody unfair life is that she's got the one she doesn't want and hasn't got the one that she does. She's used to this kind of thing in her soap, of course she is, but in a soap you have to have that kind of thing for the plot, to fill out the story, it's all been explained to her, she understands all of that, but this is real life! She doesn't want this kind of thing happening in real life! She is so miserable, so fed-up. It feels so bad that Serena thinks it must be love. She's not quite sure what love is, never having loved anyone before, but any feeling which causes her not to worry about her nails and which cover she's on is so unnatural that she can only imagine that's what she's in. Love.

Serena has never had an emotion without motive attached to it in her life. She hardly knows what to do with this new sensation, where to put it inside herself. She really likes this man. But why? He's going to be no use to her, he's obviously not well-off, he'll have no good contacts, he's not a celebrity, he isn't even a plastic surgeon. He's not going to do her career any bloody good at all. Even though she knows it's totally stupid, she can't help herself; she adores him, she wants to cuddle up to him, make him hot chocolate, massage his shoulders, and yes, even have his babies (although she won't be able to breast-feed them, not after three enlargements). She wonders how long it would take to divorce James and marry Marlon. Gareth will be furious, of course, about her hitching up with an unknown, especially as he's just told her she's not famous enough as it is. But she doesn't care – this is the sort of thing you do when you're really properly in love. You do silly, mad sorts of things which fly in the face of the demands of your media profile. She imagines Marlon, going down on his knee, asking her to be his bride, she imagines her lace wedding gown with a 30 foot train, she imagines their wedding night with that delicious body, taut and proud and perfect on top of her, ready to mount her, his young muscles straining to penetrate her to the very core. She feels her body shudder with excitement and frustration and nervous tension and reaches for her make-up bag.

The afternoon and evening come and go. How much

blusher can one face take? By 10 pm Serena gives up. James is obviously not going out. It's been a whole day wasted – a day is a long time in her business – and for all she knows Marlon's already been snapped up by someone else now and made a life-long photogenic commitment to them instead of her. She considers the possibility of waiting until James is asleep and then stealing out after dark and going to Marlon's flat. But it's started raining and suddenly the prospect of going out in the cold, wet night and having her hair go all curly in the damp somehow doesn't feel like such a good idea after all. Serena cleanses, exfoliates, buffs, tones and moisturises and, resolving that maybe true love can wait until the morning, turns off the bedside light.

*

On the way to the petrol station James decides that in the morning he'll drive round to Geraldine's and deliver the card personally instead of sending it and take a bunch of flowers with him. She'll love a romantic gesture like that plus he might get a shag out of her. But when he gets to the garage shop the only flowers they have left are the ones sprayed blue and green. Why do people think anyone wants to buy flowers which have been sprayed blue and green? Don't they notice that the ones sprayed blue and green are always the last ones left in the buckets? James wonders absent-mindedly as he randomly grabs a bunch and ambles into the shop. Choosing a card is more difficult because there's a choice. There are some which are 'blank – for your own message'. James finds the prospect of having to construct his own message rather daunting, so he shuffles further along the shelf to the cards which say it all for you. He checks over the gamut of emotive opportunities available. Congratulations; commiserations; sympathy; sorry. 'Sorry you've lost your job.' 'Sorry you failed your exam.' 'Sorry I forgot your birthday.' 'Sorry we argued.' Sorry is what he's after – women love it when a man apologises. He selects that last one, the 'Sorry we argued' one with a cartoon of a blue bird on the cover with a large tear in its eye. Although they hadn't technically argued there isn't a card which covers "Sorry I was going to dump you but then I changed my mind". Then he hesitates. Actually, now he comes to think of it, he may have forgotten Geraldine's birthday last month. Should he buy the "Sorry I forgot your birthday" card as well and present her with both of them, as part of a general "Sorry for everything I've ever done wrong ever" campaign? Maybe not. He starts to feel guilty and decides he will get a blank one after all and make the effort to write something himself. He has to wait forever in the queue to pay – there is only one girl serving. Then he finds a place in the corner of the shop where he can write the message. This is the difficult bit of course – saying something personal and meaningful. But to his annoyance, when he delivers the card from its dusty cellophane wrapper there is already a poem printed inside. He stomps back to the till. 'Look here,' he complains to the girl. 'I bought this card because it said it was blank inside so I could write a personal greeting of my own and there's already a poem in here!'

'You'll have to join the queue,' she intones indifferently, not even looking up.

'But I've just stood 10 minutes in the bloody queue to buy this! You should deal with me now!'

The girl stops serving and looks out for support and guidance from the other customers already waiting in the bloody queue who give subtle indications that they are less than happy with this suggestion. Someone tells her to ignore him and just carry on with serving them, another yelps to James that he'll deal with him himself if he doesn't go to the back of the queue.

Jesus Christ, don't these people realise who I am? he thinks.

'My name is James Marlborough,' he says. They stare at him with indifferent eyes; he could be the Easter Bunny for all they cared.

'And my wife,' he splutters nervously, 'is the actress – Serena Dawlish.'

Shock. Astonishment. Oooh, ooh, they go. Ooh. The waves part. He glides effortlessly to the front of the queue. Now there is total silence, the customers stop muttering, they stop breathing: they want to hear every word.

'Um,' James begins, standing once again at the front of the queue, 'yes, well, like I said, I bought this card thinking it was, you know, blank, and it's not. There's a poem in there.'

'Yeh?'

'And I wanted to write my own greeting.'

'Have you read the poem?'

'What?'

'Have you read the poem?' the girl says, fiddling with the piercings in her eyebrow which have gone septic. She lives in a squat with no electricity, no TV and she doesn't give a shit who this old fart's married to.

'Have I read it?'

'Yeh.' How thick is this old git? Why do they let old people out, why don't they just stick them all in a home somewhere so they can just get on and die quietly?

'Well, no.'

'Well, perhaps you should.' She folds her arms and juts her chin in the direction of the card, indicating to him to get on with it.

His audience is waiting. New people come into the shop, credit cards flapping, in a hurry to pay. They see the waiting crowd and join it. Anticipation is high. It is years, years since James has enjoyed an audience this ready for him.

'Er, ok,' he says. He starts to read.

'Not in your head! Out loud!' the girl commands because she's bored and she fancies a laugh.

'Oh. OK,' James obeys. He finds a position, takes a deep breath and reads the poem out loud, slowly, evenly.

For a while, when he has finished, no one speaks.
It is a beautiful poem. It is beautiful.
James looks up. The eyes before him are now full of tears. James clears his throat. 'I'll, er, keep the card,' he mutters and makes his exit.

CHAPTER 7

Geraldine's head is still very sore. She has spent all of the previous day in bed trying to recover from concussion and what feels like at least a couple of broken ribs. What was she thinking of, climbing up that wisteria? Risking her life for that cheating bastard! Yes, it would have been fun to have appeared at his bedroom window to see his enormous white bottom moving up and down, in and out of his wife; to have enjoyed the look on his face as he turned to behold Geraldine waving cheerfully at him. But it wasn't worth breaking her neck for it.

No, Geraldine reflects as she prepares to get ready for the interview with Serena's mother, no man is worth that much. And, now that she comes to think of it, James' bottom really is rather repulsive. Not just white, almost grey in fact, that weary shade of skin which has never seen the sun and has gone the colour of old knickers washed too many times in a hot wash with other colours. And spotty, full of those tiny angry red bumps which look like plucked chicken skin. Why would she want to see that? Why had she ever wanted to see that?

In the meantime she has a TV programme to present and the show must go on even with a violent migraine. Although it is against Geraldine's religion to leave London unless en route to Stratford, Bath or a rather yummy country house hotel she knows just the other side of Burford, she tucks Beckett in her vintage coupe MG Roadster and taps Gerrards Cross – yes, Gerrards Cross, for Christ's sake – into her sat-nav.

It takes bloody ages to get out of London and leaving an hour later than she should have done doesn't help either. When she finally arrives the crew, of course, are already waiting for her and are busy setting up lights and microphones on the pavement. But the moment she sees Mrs Dawlish's house in the distance — call it second sight, third eye, sixth sense, what you will — as soon as Geraldine draws up to the house, even before she gets out of the car, she has a bad feeling about this one.

She can see a woman out in the front garden. Her practised eye looks immediately for something that will stand out on camera. The house is just a featureless double-fronted pre-war property in Gerrards Cross. It is not grand, it is not humble, neither period nor modern. The woman is just a middle-aged woman, a woman who is not short but not tall, not old and not young, not fat but not thin, just totally dull. Both the house and the woman are nothing more and nothing less than what they are. Each of them, in their own special way, is as spectacularly bland as they can possibly be. Televisually they are a complete bloody disaster.

The woman is on her hands and knees gardening. When Geraldine looks more closely she realises that she is cutting the grass round the edges of the hideously ornate kidney-shaped bed of begonias with a pair of nail scissors.

Jesus. If you're going to be weird, at least make a bold statement that's going to look good on screen.

She lets Beckett out of the car. It's been a long drive from Islington and he instantly trots off to relieve his bowels on Mrs Dawlish's front lawn, although fortunately she has her back to him at that time. With Beckett then safely back in the car Geraldine drives round to a side street, parks the car and, only mildly trespassing through a couple of the neighbours' gardens, finds her way into Mrs Dawlish's back garden where a patio door is wide open. Geraldine quickly goes in to see if the interior of the house is any better.

She wanders forlornly from room to room. It is all hideous, especially the sitting room which is the sort of room created for guests by the sort of people who never have any. The walls are painted in that vile white with a hint of green so popular amongst those bereft of taste, the sort of white which looks like white suffering a bilious attack; they are further distressed by a selection of dismal paintings of wasteland scenes, the kind of place which only stunted clumps of gorse and the inbred inhabit. The room is sparsely furnished with a piano and a three piece suite in a particularly vibrant shade of puce, a colour which Geraldine has not seen since her student days when she contracted dysentery in Goa.

There is nothing here that will be of any use, nothing telegenic, only a dreary house occupied by a dreary woman who will do nothing for the ratings. Appalled, Geraldine flops onto the vile sofa and calls Gareth, Serena's manager.

'Listen, Gareth,' she instructs imperiously, 'it's a no-go with Serena's mother doing the part of mother on the show. She's simply too fucking boring.' Geraldine goes on to explain how awful the house is and how the woman herself is worse and Gareth starts to whinge about contractual clauses and caveats. Really the man has been a pain ever since she first started negotiating with him. He thinks because he manages Serena Dawlish he has quasi-divine status. She suffers him even though she has more intellectual capacity in her ear lobes than he enjoys anywhere between his. As he witters on, Geraldine notices a file marked 'Church Charity Fund' on the coffee table in front of her and a letter on top of it from some woman in Brentford.

'Thank you for replying to my ad with your kind offer of help what I am herewith replying to now. My name is Shelley Drayton. Until I was 9 I lived with my mum and dad. They had a big argument over whether it's better to have an upright or a cylinder vacuum cleaner and got a divorce after that. After that they made it up and went for a romantic reunion holiday in Torremolinos. It was when they was flying back from that holiday that their plane crashed into the white cliffs of Dover and they both died horrible slow deaths. I was so happy I was going to have my mum and dad back but when that plane crashed so did all my hopes of happiness and

I ended up doing drugs and alcohol – can you truly blame me? Now I got 5 kids what I have to bring up alone. My job at the factory where I make those fleecy bits what go inside slippers don't give us enough to live on. Each of their fathers of the children promised me on their mother's life that they would stay with me but in the end they all scarpered. Do not judge me too harsh for my promiscuality – I am only a poor woman what craves love and affection and men only give you that if they have sex first. Please help any way what you can.'

With the phone still stuck to her ear and Gareth still whining down it, Geraldine takes the letter from the top of the folder and slips back through the patio doors.

'And even if I could persuade my client to drop her mother from the show,' Gareth protests, 'who do you propose as a suitable replacement? Who is there who is sufficiently interesting to guarantee a better return on media spend for the show? Who can you possibly find at such short notice – the show goes out live this evening!'

'I think I know someone,' Geraldine smiles, getting back in her car and commanding the crew to pack everything up and head east to Brentford.

*

Shelley is back at the kitchen table trying to concentrate on writing that morning's letter but Marlon keeps hovering round the place, clutching at that bloody brooch, glancing across at the front door. She had hoped if no more was said about it the situation would sort itself out but she can see now that simply isn't going to happen so she decides to take the bull by the horns.

'What d'you keep looking at the door for, love?'

'Nothing,' he says miserably.

'You still thinking about that woman?'

'You mean alien. I've told you, she's an alien.'

'OK, the alien, are you still thinking about her?'

'Yes. She said she wants to sex me. I think it's what alien women do to human men. What does it mean, mum?'

Shelley looks at him. 'Sex. Right. Did we never get round to talking about that?'

'No.'

'Right. OK. Sex. Well, it's hard to know where to start really . . .' She is just attempting to grope for the right words when suddenly Marlon screams and points to the cover of that week's issue of 'Turn Me On' magazine on the kitchen table. 'There she is!' he cries. 'The alien! The alien who is after me!'

Fucking hell, thinks Shelley. He's even worse than I thought. Those E's they put in fishfingers, they've got a lot to answer for.

'Don't be daft, love. That's Serena Dawlish, the actress what's Sue Upton in "Coombe Ridge Crescent". You never want to watch TV any more otherwise you'd know that!'

'That's her, I tell you!' Marlon interrupts. 'That's the alien who wants to sex me!'

Shelley's powerful shoulders slump with relief. 'Oh, that's OK then,' she smiles.

'Is it?'

'Yeh. Course it is. It's natural. You and half the country, the male half, they're all having fantasies about being abducted by her. It's a sign you're normal. You've nothing to worry about.'

'So you don't mind she's coming to get me?'

'Not if it makes you happy, love.'

'Because she was meant to be here at 3 o'clock yesterday and even though she didn't turn up then I'm sure she'll be coming soon. To come and, you know, sex me.'

'Course she will.'

'You don't believe me?'

'What? That Serena Dawlish, Britain's most famous actress, is really an alien and, any minute now, she's like gonna, what, just turn up on the doorstep and say, "Hi Marlon, it's me, I've come for you"? Is that what you're asking me to believe?'

As she speaks a woman's face appears between the plastic net daisy pattern lace curtains at the kitchen window.

Marlon freezes and stares.

'That's her. She's out there.'

'Yeh. Her, Santa and the tooth fairy. They've all come for tea.'

'Don't be daft, mum,' Marlon says. 'Santa and the tooth fairy don't exist.'

The doorbell rings. He opens the door.

A woman says, 'Hi Marlon, it's me.'

Shelley staggers back. It is Serena Dawlish; it is Sue Upton. Standing there on the concrete walkway right outside her own front door is Shelley's other self, her alter-ego, her pretend her, the woman she would be if only she was slimmer, younger, braver, wiser, prettier, luckier than she actually is. It's the woman she's spent all this time watching on the telly, imagining she was her, beautiful like her, living in a big house with stacks of money and everything just as it should be.

'My God, you're me,' Shelley says.

Serena takes one look at the large thing in front of her.

'My God, I really don't think so,' she replies. She stares at Marlon. He looks more gorgeous than ever. She takes in his fabulous body, his chiselled jaw, his hairy chest showing at the top of his shirt, the gorgeous green eyes, especially the right one with the brown flecks – he's irresistible. 'I told you I'd come for you and here I am,' she gurgles.

'Yes,' says Marlon. 'I knew you'd come eventually. I'm ready for you.' He takes his jacket and makes to go.

Suddenly Shelley is terrified. How can this just be coincidence? How can it all have worked out this way and how can Marlon have seen it coming? Maybe if this is true then everything else that Marlon has ever told her might also be true. Maybe the aliens do exist. The microwave, the ELF rays, Roswell, it might all be just like he says it is. The brooch and the funny squiggles on the television, maybe it was all true.

Maybe this woman really is an alien come to abduct her baby and this is goodbye to her darling son, the son she has loved and nurtured and cherished every moment of his existence.

All at once Shelley comes to a decision – it doesn't matter how famous she is, this bitch isn't taking her boy!

'He's going nowhere,' Shelley says firmly putting her stomach roundly between Serena and the object of their desire.

'And who are you to tell him what he can and can't do?'

'I'm his mum!'

Serena looks at the blob in a nighty big enough to double as a king-size duvet. 'Did you adopt?'

'No! Why?'

'Never mind. Come on, Marlon, let's go.' She holds out her hand – each hovering finger straining with the weight of a long curling talon decorated in green and black stripes.

'I mean it,' Shelley says, suppressing a slight belch which doesn't suit the moment but those salt'n'vinegar crisps she had for breakfast always repeat on her terribly. 'You ain't taking my boy.'

'Boy? He's a grown man!'

'Not to me he ain't.'

'Just because you're his mother doesn't mean you can go throwing your weight around like this!' Serena yells indignantly with the emphasis on the word 'weight'. 'You need to let go, you know. It's psychological!'

'Don't lecture me about psychological!' Shelley retorts angrily. 'I'm five foot five and 18 stone! I know more about psychological than you ever will!'

'She's right,' Marlon whispers to Shelley. 'You've got to let me go, mum. It's my destiny, you know it is.'

Serena raises a victorious plucked eyebrow. Shelley knows she's got to think quickly.

'Tell you what, why don't you come in for a minute and we'll have a cup of tea and sort this one out?'

'In – here?'

'Yeh. Marlon can show you his big telescope, Miss Dawlish. Can't you, Marlon love? And I'll make tea and arrange Penguin biscuits in a pattern on a plate,' Shelley offers enthusiastically. She has to stop this thing going any further but right now she can't come up with any way of stopping it so she'd better keep Serena here till she can. Best to act friendly until she's got a plan sorted.

Serena has a think about it. Maybe it would be better to do it here rather than her place just in case James changes his mind and does come back up to the bedroom.

'OK,' she sighs.

'Lovely. And I'll put the kettle on!' Shelley says, obviously pleased, standing aside to let Serena pass.

Marlon leads her gently by the hand – oh, the feel of his large warm hand on hers! – into a small kitchen which is probably the most horrible room Serena's ever been in. Everything is yellow, the floor, the walls, the ceiling, the cabinets. Nothing is fashionable and everything is cheap. At this stage of her career she really doesn't want to know that places like this actually exist, much less go into them. She's seen them on the sets of 'Coombe Ridge Crescent', which is fine, it's TV. This isn't TV. She's really here, for Christ's sake. In a place where the net curtains are made of plastic and the work surfaces aren't granite, where the fridge isn't integrated and where the kitchen taps aren't uniflow. This is all horrible and not designer at all. Suddenly she feels so depressed. She starts to shake and feel ill. How cruel life is that it's taken all this time for her to find true love and now that she has, his kitchen doesn't even have an espresso machine.

From there he takes her through to a sitting room which looks like a science lab, full of telescopes and cameras and computers and notebooks.

'I suppose this is what you want to see,' Marlon announces with a mixture of pride and fear. 'What is it you're after? My notebooks with all my calculations, my equipment?'

'Ooh, you know I want your equipment, babe!'

'Yes, I know that,' Marlon says flatly. 'Well, I'm not sure where to start, there's so much stuff in here. This is my biggest telescope,' he explains. 'I have five – my mother gets me whatever I need.'

'What do you do with all of this?' Serena asks blankly. She's just embarrassed really. She doesn't expect a man who offers to show her his big telescope really to have one.

'Well,' says Marlon, wondering if this is a trick question of some sort, 'obviously I use it to see, you know, where you come from.'

She looks confused.

'You can see Gerrards Cross through here?'

What's Gerrards Cross, he wonders? He decides it must be the name she gives to the symbol with the cross he saw on the TV screen, the one on the brooch she gave him. 'Yes, that's where I saw it first.'

'Blimey. It must be a good telescope if you can see all the way up the M40 with it.'

'Would you like to look through it?' he asks. 'Of course you won't see anything now. You need to be here at night when there are no clouds in the sky. At night I could show you how to do it. I could show you how to read the messages the stars send us. Because they communicate with us all the time, you know, they talk to us, they tell us what we need to know. They told me you were coming. They did. I've known it for a while now. I saw it all in the night sky.'

He smiles at her, such a lovely, sexy smile. Jesus, what a smile – he really is drop-dead bloody gorgeous. He talks a lot of crap but he looks so good! She can see him now on her arm at the National Television Awards, his face would fill a TV camera perfectly. She must be brave and persevere. It all feels so hard, so unnatural but perhaps this is what real love is like – ridiculous, imperfect but worth it in the end? She must give it a try, she must.

She approaches the telescope and looks through it.

'This is the best time to see things at night – with a new moon following the vernal equinox. But then, of course, you must know much more about that kind of thing than I do,' he says.

Serena tries her best to see something through the telescope, adjusting the position of her head this way and that, but it's impossible, her false eyelashes keep getting in the way.

Marlon, meanwhile, is watching her beautiful body as it curves over the telescope. He is thinking about that sexing thing and starting to fret. What, exactly, will it involve? Will it hurt? When are they going to do it? Will she tell him when they're going to do it or will she suddenly just start doing it? Will he even know when she's started?

'What about the sex thing?' he asks.

Serena smiles. 'You bet,' she says. She turns towards him and kisses him. Suddenly her hand is back where it was in the car, between his legs. Marlon can feel the blood rushing to his head. He feels giddy, disoriented, faint. This is the sex thing then. This is what she's got planned for him. Some special twist of her wrist that affects his central nervous system and makes him feel like he's about to pass out. His self-control is floating further and further away. All that exists is her hand rubbing back and forth up and down between his legs; he can feel her lovely body pressing against him; he can taste the sweetness of her mouth; he can smell the cheese on toast.

Cheese on toast?

He breaks away from Serena's embrace – his mother is standing next to them balancing a large tray laden with food and drink.

'I've brought cheese on toast, Miss Dawlish,' Shelley offers pleasantly, 'what, as you will soon find out, is my son's favourite snack. Just as well you start to get to know his little ways, eh? Crusts cut off of course and tomato ketchup under the cheese before it's put on the grill. Don't worry, you'll soon learn! He's an easy boy, really, when you get used him,' she adds cheerfully. She settles the tray on an attractive faux mahogany sideboard and sorts out the cutlery. 'Let me tell you, Miss Dawlish,' she chatters happily as she works, 'it's so nice that my Marlon's finally brought a young lady back. I was beginning to despair that he'd ever have a girlfriend. Oh, don't get me wrong, I'm not implying he's ever been of the other persuasion, no! But he's always been so hung up with his astronomy stuff that he's never bothered with the girls. You two been having fun?' she adds nervously as she turns and sees the look on their faces.

'We were trying to,' Serena replies coldly.

'Right,' Shelley says.

They all stand and stare at the plates of congealing cheddar.

Suddenly Shelley bursts into tears. 'The thing is, I don't really think I can stand it, you taking my boy away, I really don't think I can. He means everything to me, he's my life, my prince, my baby!'

Serena stares at her. What does she care what this fat woman's feelings are?

Marlon is a man so he does nothing but stand and wait and hope that the difficult emotional moment will soon pass.

Shelley sobs, a small trickle of wet wending its way down over her upper lip.

Suddenly Serena has doubts. She does fancy this Marlon like mad but his mum is starting to give her the creeps. Plus she's just too big for words – not a little bit fat like the way Serena gets after a few days if she has too much marmalade on her toast in the morning, but really properly revoltingly fat with rolls and blubber and chins and stomachs and everything. She must be at least a size 18. What would that look like in the wedding photos? And the magazine articles? His mother will take up a double page spread all by herself! Yes, Serena is in love with Marlon but there's the visuals, the marketing, the strategy to think of. If Gareth's taught her one thing he's taught her that.

Gareth — that's who she needs. She needs his advice. She needs to know what she's letting herself in for here, whether she can go ahead with this falling in love thing or not.

'Hang on a sec,' she says. She grabs her mobile phone. 'Gareth? Hi, it's me. Look, the thing is, I don't think you're going to like this but I'm about to have an affair. Er, he's called Marlon. Marlon Drayton. Well, no, you won't have heard of him because no one has. Why not? Oh, God, listen, Gareth, it's complicated. He's not, well, oh God, how can I say this, he's not famous. No. No! I've told you. No! That's right — not even a tiny bit. No, no, he's not rich either. But the thing is, I was thinking, Gareth — as I'm so famous couldn't he sort of just be famous for being with me? I mean, wouldn't it sort of be an advantage in a way to be with someone not as famous as me so he won't try to compete with me for space in the photos? What? Hang on, I'll ask him.'

She holds the phone aside. 'Can you play a musical instrument? Or sing?'

Marlon shakes his head.

She goes back to the phone.

'That's a no, Gareth. What? Hang on, I'll ask him.'

She asks Marlon: 'Do you play football or are you a politician?'

Once again, Marlon slowly hangs his head and shakes it.

'No, Gareth, no. What does he do? Well, he does stars. No! Not like that. He looks at them, you know, the ones in the sky. Through a telescope, well five really. Yes. That is all he does.'

At this point Gareth's voice can be heard yelling, 'I've told you, Serena, your fame isn't even enough for you any more, much less enough to start handing it out to any talentless loser you happen to pick up!'

'But, Gareth, you don't understand — I love him!'

At this point Gareth loses his already tried patience and

starts to shout, very loudly, and to use lots of words which suggest displeasure. So as not to cause her inner lobes permanent damage, Serena holds the mobile away from her ear for the duration of Gareth's rant. This unfortunately means that Marlon and his mother also hear Gareth's hearty recommendations that over his dead fucking body he's going to let her bloody well mess up all the work he's sodding well invested in her for some unknown fucking saddo unemployed dossing arsehole but what can Serena do? She can't keep her ear glued to that kind of a racket. She's got very delicate hearing, it's a hereditary thing she got from her mother, it's not her fault.

When, eventually, Gareth calms down, she goes back to the phone. 'Yes, I'm with him now. No, no, we haven't done anything yet. No, no photographers, I'm sure of that. Yes, yes, my career, I understand. But Gareth – what about love?'

'Love?' he barks. 'What's that got to do with anything? I don't know what's got into you – you know your career's on the line as it is and you want to jeopardise everything by hitching up with this complete unknown. It's preposterous. If this is your attitude I may have to think about terminating my relationship with you. I'm doing my very best here to keep you afloat and you're intent on ruining it all. Is this how you want to repay me for my efforts, is it?, with this absurd act of sentimental folly?'

'No,' Serena mumbles. She thinks for a while. 'What if I just have him as a lover, just for the sex – people do that, don't they?'

'Don't be absurd. A woman can't do that. My male clients can get away with having a bit on the side, it makes them virile. It would just make you a slut and you can imagine what the advertisers would think about that.'

Gareth's right, of course, Serena knows that. At 12.75 per cent, in fact now 17.75 per cent, of all her earnings he should be bloody right. Even so, the thought of never seeing Marlon again makes her want to cry more of those real tear thingies but Gareth hears them coming and warns her they'll give her bags under the eyes. She's a celebrity, he bellows, can't she just accept that? She doesn't have a normal life with feelings and needs and shit like that. What she does she does to be famous; more famous; as famous as she can possibly be. The sooner she understands it the better.

Serena flips shut the phone and feels the tears come, even with the worry about the bags under her eyes and even though there's no one there to film them. She turns to Marlon.

'I'm so sorry, Marlon. I'm so, so sorry. I do fancy you. I really do. But Gareth, that's my manager, he says, well, you heard what he said. He doesn't think it would be a good idea. He agrees entirely that at this stage of my career, what with my fitness DVD just out and everything, I should leave James, my husband, and get maximum exposure from that, but not to go to an unknown with no potential. Gareth is my manager, Marlon. I've got to listen to him. I pay him 17.75 per cent of everything I earn!'

Marlon hasn't understood a word of what Serena has just said.

'What are you saying? Are you saying my boy isn't good enough for you?' Shelley cries.

'Listen,' says Serena to Marlon, ignoring her, 'You have to believe me, there's nothing I'd like more than to have an on-off affair with you, take you as my live-in lover, get engaged, separate then have a romantic tearful reunion, be supported by you through a messy divorce then marry you in pink lace in a secret ceremony witnessed only by close family and photographers from a magazine. But I'm a celebrity, Marlon! Do you understand what that means? It means I have a public and a responsibility to my public. I'm recognised wherever I go. I have an image I must project. Oh, this is all so hard! I really do fancy you, I mean I fancy the balls off you but what can I do? What can I do?!'

The tears are running down her cheeks now, forging furrows down through the blusher and foundation and below the eye luminiser and skin enhancing light reflecting cheekbone highlighter. Genuine emotion is all so new to Serena and now she's having so much of it in one day.

'How dare you say my boy ain't good enough for you! My boy's worth a thousand of what you are! If you leave him I'll sort you out! I'll go to the papers, ruin your career!' Shelley screams.

'You'll go to the papers? Get real! No one's going to take any notice of you. You're not famous, you don't count. Even worse, you're fat – who's going to listen to you?'

She gives Marlon one last lingering kiss and Shelley one last withering look. 'And you – you're not even getting an autograph!' she snarls at her as she departs.

From the window Marlon watches Serena running across to her waiting car. That sex thing – even if it was going to kill him he can think of worse ways to die. He sees her slender legs, her long silky hair, her massive breasts rising and falling with each step. He feels his crotch knot harder with desire. He knows what she has done. She has infiltrated his system. She must have passed a secretion through to him, probably when their mouths were open onto each other, which has altered his chemical state.

He goes back to his desk in the lounge. He tries to focus on his maths and his notebooks and the trajectories of the stars projected against the evolution of prime numbers but the fact is that he no longer gives a monkey's about any of that. All he can think about is the smell of the alien's neck and her long legs and the curve of her breasts and the way her fingers felt as they were winding their way round his penis. She has poisoned him in some way, infected his skin, his marrow, his blood stream, so he no longer has the will to carry out his work. This is no doubt the first step in her plan to mutate his DNA for her own needs. She has done her job well. His whole body is now electric with the longing to see her again – to see her and do more of those things they were doing before his mum came in. But then of course if he does more of that with the alien she will have an even stronger hold on him. This is obviously her tactic. What is Marlon to do? He is doomed, doomed. He had such good intentions, to save the world, to make his mother proud – now all he can think of is the touch of the alien woman's hands working their way up his thighs.

Shelley should be pleased but she's not. Yes, it's all over between him and Serena Dawlish, she's got her boy back but look what it's done to him – his heart is broken. He's sitting with his head down on his desk, his eyes shut, his notebooks unopened.

'Eat your cheese on toast,' she says tenderly to him. 'It'll help take away the pain.'

★

Serena's just got into her car when Gareth rings her back and tells her he wants her in his office asap. All the way there Serena hopes against hope that he might be going to say he's found a way for her to be with Marlon after all, a way for her to be in love without it having a detrimental effect on her optimum earnings and exposure potential. How's she going to bring up the subject without Gareth going ape again? But when she arrives, to her delight, he's the one who does.

'About what you were saying earlier on the phone, that man,'

'Marlon?'

'Yes, well, that's what I wanted to talk to you about.'

'It is?' Serena exclaims brightly.

'Yes. I've been giving it some thought and perhaps you're right – it's a good idea.'

'Oh Gareth, thank you, you don't know how happy you've made me!'

'Not with him of course, he sounds like a total loser, but

I've done some calculations on my spreadsheet and I think that the idea, the idea is good. Even if you don't leave James, you should have an affair at this stage, a public one that is, otherwise people are going to worry that you're sexually under par.'

'Who's Par?'

'Your public needs to see more of the sexual side of you off set as well as on. So I've got something arranged for you, a lover. He's here now, in one of the offices next door.'

'What? Already?'

'This is a fast-moving business, Serena. It's all set up, everything's in place, you two are officially an item as of now.'

Serena is appalled. 'Gareth! Hello! What if I don't fancy him! You can't expect me to just see him and want to do it with him! What if I don't like the look of him?!'

'Oh no, I haven't made things clear. You don't have to actually do anything with him, just be seen in public together, holding hands, having lunches, going into hotels, coming out of hotels, generally provoking lots of column inches of intense media speculation.'

'Why would I do that? Why would he do that?'

'I've come to an arrangement with his manager. You need visibility and exposure. And he needs help with his career too.'

'What kind of help?'

'Well, don't you want to know who it is first?'

'Yes, of course!'

Gareth calls through to his secretary to bring him through. Moments later in walks a short, bald man in his fifties. 'Oh no way, Gareth,' Serena cries out immediately, 'no fucking way!'

'This is John, Alex Cordell's manager. And this,' says Gareth, indicating the man who walks in behind him, 'is Alex Cordell.'

'Alex Cordell!' Serena gasps. She feels her chest swell, her heart thud, her pupils dilate, everything happening that needs to happen when a woman experiences strong physical desire for a man. Alex Cordell – only the best looking man on television! And not even in soap but proper TV drama, the highest art form there is! Why, only last week he'd been in a two hour drama spectacular with double-length ads where he was the detective who made the female suspect fall in love with him. (Like there was ever any doubt she was going to do that!)

Alex Cordell looks very bored to be there. He is wearing a smart navy blue suit and a white T-shirt with 'BUM' written in glitter across the chest. He is so cool. He is so beautiful. Serena feels the dribble collecting at the corners of her mouth. He barely acknowledges her. He sits and picks at invisible bits of fluff on the sleeves of his suit. He must be shy. He's got lovely hands, Serena notices, nicely manicured nails. Why don't more men take care of their nails? His hair is beautifully coloured – Serena knows a good colour when she sees one. His tan is great, just the right tone of gold. She'd have so much in common with a man like this, she can tell. They could share beauticians, compare notes on depilation and Botox. She gives him a smile to let him know the impression he's making is favourable. He takes out his Blackberry and starts tapping away at it in between picking off more invisible fluff.

Meanwhile the managers finalise terms. They talk about the media-purposes-only romantic attachment clauses, strategic photo opportunities, tactical nudity – all stuff that goes way above Serena's head and anyway, she's too upset to take it any more.

Yes. Upset. Because suddenly this is more than Serena can bear. She has to go to the ladies room and re-do her make-up to give herself the strength to cope. Why does destiny do this to her? People say you have to wait ages for a bus and then two come along at once and it's true, it's so true! She's coming over all philosophical but can you blame her? Just when she's found the love of her life suddenly there's another man in the picture who's perfect for her career and she's got a real dilemma. It's so unfair. Now she's really being put to the test. It's a crossroads in her life. One day she will look back at this moment and think – did I make the right decision? I had two paths I could follow – did I choose the right one? On the one hand I could follow my heart, on the other my vocation. On the one hand emotional happiness, on the other success, money, fame. And this Alex Cordell, he's bound to fall in love with her, he probably is already madly in love with her, that's why he's agreed to do this deal and even though it's only meant to be for media purposes, before she knows it Alex Cordell will be proposing to her and wanting life-long commitment from her and then she'll never be able to have Marlon, never!

Life is so cruel. Happiness is so that f-ing thing Gareth said.

She applies one final layer of foundation, just to give her the courage she needs. Then she walks back into office.

Gareth is there, alone.

'Where are the others?' Serena exclaims.

'They've gone. It was really just a matter of getting their signatures on the contract, it had all been decided in advance really. Now I just need yours.' He hands her a pen.

She sighs. 'So, it's come to this, Gareth. You want me to sign a piece of paper to say I will have an affair with Alex Cordell. You're asking me to sacrifice my body for my career. OK,' she sighs again, 'I suppose it's something I'll just have to do for my art . . .'

'What? No, no, Serena, you still don't understand. You're really not going to have to do anything with Alex. This affair is just for publicity.'

'What? You mean I won't, like, you know, have sex with him?'

'Oh no, not at all. Alex is gay. He's just been offered the lead in a new series "Ravished" in which he plays a heartless womaniser who cons wealthy widows and divorcees out of their money. He just needs to protect his image until that's over then he's going to come out and star in a new series called "Straight Up" about a vulnerable actor who reveals to the world he's gay. It's all about timing, Serena, you know that. Meanwhile he's so high-profile that he'll give your image a real boost. Not enough to make you famous enough forever but just famous enough for now.'

'Excuse me, what about when he comes out? People'll think it's been sex with me that's put him off being normal!'

Gareth studies her with contempt. 'Being gay is perfectly normal,' he says slowly.

'So all I have to do is pretend I'm sleeping with him?'

'You've got it,' Gareth concludes with relief. 'You're meeting him for a drink this evening. I've got a schedule here for how your affair is going to progress after that.'

He pushes the contract under her nose and she signs it. She wants to ask about Marlon, ask whether he's really sure there's no hope but the look on Gareth's face tells her she needn't bother.

'There's one other thing before you go. The producer of tonight's show has rung to say that your mother is too boring to be your mother. Apparently she went to your mother's house to interview her this morning, took one look at her and decided she's simply too dull.'

'Right,' mumbles Serena indifferently. She doesn't care about the show or Gareth or her mother. All she cares about is Marlon.

Gareth drones on, advising Serena that she absolutely has to follow this woman's professional advice in the interest of her career. The good news is that a new, more televisually exciting mother has already been found for her and Serena will meet her on the show. Will Serena, in the meantime, ring her mother to tell her she's just not right for the part of mother?

*

James is about to set off with the card and the flowers to Geraldine's to let her know he's all hers. Just before he goes he puts in a quick call to his divorce lawyer, who is an old drinking pal, to tell him that he's going to leave Serena and ask him to put things in motion to that effect.

The lawyer takes a few moments to talk James through the financial implications of being true to his heart.

It's at this point James realises just how much his marriage really means to him. Serena may have her shadow sides but don't we all? Now that he actually thinks about it he can't bring himself to leave her. He just couldn't put her through that amount of pain. Yes, he'll do the honourable thing. He'll stay with her. It's the morally correct thing to do.

He'll give the card and flowers to her instead.

James rings Geraldine back and leaves another message. He says he's thought things through and he's realised he cannot be so selfish. She is a talented, beautiful woman about to embark on an exciting new career. He can't hold her back with his selfish needs. In short it is only because he loves her so very much that, in spite of all the other texts and messages he left her yesterday, he's going to have to be strong and let her go.

*

Serena has her first rendezvous with Alex Cordell. All they have to do is meet for a surreptitious lunch-time drink at one of the most prominent tables at The Wolseley in Piccadilly. She's feeling nervous and rings Gareth en route.

'Tell me it's all going to be OK, Gareth. I mean, I know this is meant to be for media purposes only and everything but what if he falls madly in love with me and I have to fend him off?'

'No chance,' says Gareth.

'No chance?' she squeals. 'This is me, Gareth. You know the effect I have on men!'

'Not this one. I've told you. He's gay.'

'How can you be sure? I mean some people say they're gay but it's just a phase they're going through. They grow out of it.'

'And some say they are because they are. And I know Alex is because I've had sex with him myself.'

'Don't be daft, Gareth,' says Geraldine. 'That would mean you're gay!'

'Yes,' says Gareth.

'Omigod,' says Serena, 'I'm so sorry. I didn't know. Have you been it long?'

'It?'

'Gay.'

'Er, yes. Always.'

'Oh dear. I'm sorry. Have you got used to it now?'

'Yes.'

'Your parents must be so upset.'

'They're coping.'

'So you can give me advice, I mean, how does it work, can gay men suddenly be converted back to normal if they're exposed to a sexy enough woman? Can that happen?'

'No.'

'OK, well, I mean, it might though. Alex Cordell might spend some time with me and suddenly get better.'

Gareth hangs up.

Alex Cordell meets Serena, has a quick, surreptitious, public drink, is photographed by the photographer Gareth has arranged for the occasion, then leaves, unconverted.

CHAPTER 8

Geraldine, her dog and the camera crew following her finally return to London from Gerrards Cross. When Geraldine first taps into her sat-nav the street name on the letter she took from Barbara Dawlish's house she sees, to her amazement, that it is only a couple of hundred yards from James's house in Brentford where the two of them sometimes meet for sex when his inane wife is out at work. It seems hardly feasible, she reflects, that a down-and-out could be living in almost the next street to James' superb Georgian residence in The Butts. But then of course her own home, a four bedroom penthouse apartment overlooking Gibson Square in Islington, is itself irritatingly near some unpleasant housing estates, fortunately in the other direction from Upper Street so that Geraldine never has to quite acknowledge their existence.

When she arrives at Shelley Drayton's block of flats Geraldine has to suppress a small shiver of excitement. It is part of an estate of a squalid council blocks, a construct of pitted bricks the colour of rust lined with black mortar. The windows are small, occasional; they appear inserted as an afterthought when someone realised that the inmates would, after all, need to have some light. A long parade of wheely bins squat in dull resignation either side of the entrance like soldiers guarding their fortress. There are two large boards which obliterate the scabby patch of green which poses as garden in front of the block. One which instructs 'NO PARKING' and another 'NO BALL GAMES' over which someone has scrawled the word 'CUNT' in orange paint. This is more like it, Geraldine thinks. Genuine, hard-hitting poverty. Real telegenic working-class squalor – although she's going to have to get one of the crew to remove that word from the board and replace it with something the TV censors will pass – the show's going out at 9 and there are limits. She may also ask a couple of the crew to scatter some syringes and loll around on the scruffy turf in front of the block to look like a pair of addicts, just to complete the tableau when they film their entrance to Serena Dawlish's mother's home.

At this moment Geraldine's mobile rings: it's James again. She already knows what the call is about. Yesterday when she was lying in bed not taking calls trying to recover from her fall he rang her a thousand times and left a thousand messages to tell her he wanted to leave Serena for her and could he bring his stuff round. This poses something of a dilemma for Geraldine: she can't work out whether it would be better for Serena's marriage to fall apart before or after the show. Before would give Serena an even higher profile but might at the same time make her look like a bit of a lame duck. Eventually Geraldine concludes pragmatically that it would probably be best if they were to split up after the show. She puts her phone on silent so he doesn't bother her any more during filming.

Geraldine prepares herself for the interview. Like the accomplished professional she is, she takes a few moments to put herself psychologically in the mindset of those she is about to encounter, those whose lives she is about to showcase. This is not difficult for Geraldine – she has a genuine understanding of these kind of people; she has read about them in 'The Guardian' and she once directed O'Casey's 'The Juno And The Paycock'. She can empathise with deprivation and inferiority. She knows that people of this social condition do nothing but copulate with each other and drink to dull the pain of their monotonous existences. She will have to speak quite slowly and eschew irony and metaphor and words like eschew. She parks her car under the 'NO PARKING' sign, slips off her suede Jimmy Choo courts and puts on a cheaper pair of designer shoes she keeps on the back seat for emergencies – God knows what she might tread in round here. She picks up Beckett and tucks him under her arm, she dares not leave him in the car in a place like this – he's a second generation pedigree Crufts champion Shar Pei, for Christ's sake. She can't even let him go for a wee-wee, he might put his paw on a used condom or try to eat a discarded burger – he's on a strict macrobiotic diet. He'll just have to put his bladder on hold.

*

Shelley is in her kitchen. She's got to finish a card suitable for a divorcee to her ex-husband on the occasion of his re-marriage. Personally Shelley can't see there'd be a large market for cards like that – most of the women she knows wouldn't piss on their ex's if they were on fire much less go out and spend good money on a card for them. She has to keep reminding herself that the cards she writes are not for normal people but for rich types with too much time on their hands, the sort of people what have done therapy and think that happiness and sadness and anger are all good feelings and want lots of them all the time. That's what the greetings card company told her anyway. The greetings cards people have told her she's the best one they've got on their books and they pay her more than the others. And someone out there must be buying her cards because they keep coming back for more.

Shelley puts down her pen and sighs. She works out how long she's got to wait till she can go back down the pub for today's episode of 'Coombe Ridge Crescent'. She thinks of how she can fill the time until then. Write another letter, post another letter, write another poem for another greetings card, eat. She wonders what Sue Upton must be doing now, how she's going to cope with Jenny's betrayal, how she must feel about it, what she will do for revenge – not just revenge against Jenny but that bloody Nigel who never should have ended their engagement just because he found her in bed with his dad that time, these things happen for

God's sake, it's like get over it and move on, you don't end an engagement with someone like Sue over something as daft as that!

*

Geraldine walks with the rest of the crew over the sodden clumps of ill-tempered grass which probably once passed for a lawn and enters a desolate hallway which smells vaguely of food and urine. A sign indicates that flat 5C is at the top of the stairs. Geraldine is not afraid – she has 4 large crew men to protect her – she is just annoyed that she has forgotten to bring her little piece of cloth with her she keeps in the car in case she has to sit on anything less than clean, to protect the fabric of her Dolce and Gabbana skirt. They all plod up the stairwell and then along a long covered walkway which runs outside the length of the block to a front door at the end adorned with plastic pots full of plastic flowers and plastic lace net at the window.

Geraldine rings the bell. A woman appears and lurches the door open.

'Shelley Drayton?'

'Yeh?'

Geraldine looks at her and gasps. She cannot believe her luck. However good she might have hoped this would be it is better. What Geraldine wants is someone who people will be talking about the day after the show, someone who stands out. This woman doesn't just stand out, she spills all over the place. This woman is a hulk, a colossus, an immensity. This woman is properly, horrendously huge. The sweatshirt she is wearing is so tight on her that it bulges with the bulges of her body. Her green leggings suck onto every contour. She's has a round fat head with fat curls on it. Fat hangs over the waist of the leggings all the way round like a flotation device. She'll fill the screen. She'll be incomparable, unforgettable. Who knows, there may even be a merchandising opportunity here – Shelley Drayton T-shirts, mugs, key ring fobs – the sky's the limit. This woman is made for TV. She is perfect, thinks Geraldine. Perfect, perfect, perfect.

'You sent this begging letter to a church fund in Gerrards Cross,' Geraldine says, holding up the letter in evidence. 'And I've come to see you – to give you money.'

'Lovely,' says Shelley and holds out her hand for the cash.

'Glad to see your leg is better,' Geraldine comments drily before reminding herself that she'd promised herself she wasn't doing irony here.

'You what?'

'Never mind. But listen – do you say "you what" often?'

'What?'

' "You what." You know, what you just said before you said "what" just then. Because if you do I was just wondering whether it could become a catchphrase. If you could make sure, if it is something you do say, that you say it as often as poss? That would be great. People love a catchphrase.'

The woman looks confused.

'Er, can I come in?' Geraldine asks nicely.

'What for?'

'Well, you know, just to check the place out, just to see that your life is as bad as you say it is.'

'It's not a good time right now.'

'Isn't it?'

'No.'

They stare at each other.

'All right, look, the truth is I'm a film producer and I'd like you to pretend you're Serena Dawlish's mother for a new series I'm making starting this evening called "I Gave Birth To A Celebrity".'

'You what?'

'That's it. Super. Yes. Really. I'm a TV producer. And this is my crew.'

'Are you taking the piss?'

'No. Honestly. Look at their equipment, their cameras.

Look at me. I'm obviously someone connected with the arts.'

'What's wrong with her real mum?'

'She's dead.'

'No, she ain't. I know everything about Serena Dawlish. I'm a member of her fan club and I get the newsletter every week. Her mum is called Barbara, she's 53, she lives in Gerrards Cross and she used to be a secretary at a funeral parlour.'

'That figures,' Geraldine reflects philosophically.

'But she ain't dead.'

'No, you're right, she's not dead but the thing is she's simply too boring to be in the show. I'll pay you – £500 – cash.'

'What about Serena?'

'Serena? Oh she's fine with it.'

'Is she?'

'Yes.'

'What – she knows it's me what's gonna be her TV mum?'

'No, no, she's got no idea who it is, just that it's not going to be her own mother.'

'£500?'

'Yes. Look.' Geraldine fans the notes out in front of her. One thing Geraldine learnt young – always keeps some spare cash in your handbag, you never know when it'll come in handy.

This all seems a bit strange, one minute Serena Dawlish is here trying to chat up her son, the next some telly woman's arrived saying she wants her to be Serena's mum. Nevertheless, 500 quid is 500 quid in anyone's language. 'You're on,' Shelley says. 'But I warn you,' she adds as she opens the door and lets the scrawny madwoman and her shit-faced dog into the flat, 'it's a bloody pit in here.'

'Yes, I know,' says Geraldine. 'That's why we're here.'

The crew traipse in dutifully behind her.

Geraldine looks around her. A large pile of clothes erupts majestically from the floor in the centre of the room like a piece of contemporary art. Shelley mumbles something at it and kicks it heavily to one side, sending up from its folds a medley of the danker odours of the human condition. Another pile, of plates and pans, topples aggressively in the sink and over the counters. Piles of black bin bags, full of rotting food from the stench of them, are stacked in one corner. Piles of processed food, half-open packs of chocolate biscuits, cascading white sliced bread, open-topped jars of jam, bottles half-empty with orange, curdling milk, spill out and over drawers and cupboards.

Geraldine had always thought she had a pretty good idea about what the interior of a working class house would look like. She's never actually been in one but of course she has staged them in her plays. This is the first time she's experienced one for real and it doesn't fit – it's nothing like the stage sets she's done. Her sets were neat and house-proud reflecting the psyche of those who have little but who treasure what they do own. She wonders which one's wrong – her scenery or Shelley's flat.

Anyway, the point is, this is much more interesting than bloody Barbara's suburban semi. This is going to televise a dream.

Shelley puts on the kettle, then ferrets around in the sink and finds a mug with a picture of a donkey in striped pyjamas on it. She runs some water over it then inspects it then scrapes out something from inside it with her fingernail and wipes what she's dug out onto her leggings. She shakes some instant coffee into the mug and pours the steaming water onto it. She picks up a random selection of milk bottles, sniffs them and after she has sniffed four returns to the first one and tips that into the mug. She pours a good quantity of caster sugar in from the bag and stirs it all with the handle of a knife. She has a good look, removes something from the surface of the liquid and hands it to Geraldine.

'Coffee,' she says proudly.

'Sorry but I only drink Columbian,' Geraldine says with a polite smile.

'What? You just sat there on your arse and watched me do it all, make you a coffee what was gonna be for you and you didn't bother to say nothing?' Shelley hollers.

'Tell me, do you talk like this all the time?'

'Talk like what?'

'Like you're auditioning for a bit part in "Oliver"? I mean do you occasionally stop that and start talking normally?'

'Eh? This is normal!'

'OK, super, just checking, now we need to have a little chat, you know, just so I can get an angle on you, so we can prepare for the interview.'

'What's that?' Shelley asks.

'What? An interview? It's when I ask you questions for the show.'

'No, that,' Shelley repeats, indicating Geraldine's dog which is busy sniffing at something under Shelley's fridge.

'Oh, it's my dog.'

'I know that! I know it's a dog! But has it, like, been in a car accident?'

'No!'

'So it was born looking like that?'

'Looking like what? This dog is a pedigree Shar Pei. They originated with the Han Dynasty in Dah Let near the South China Sea over two thousand years ago.'

'This dog is two thousand years old?'

'No, of course not – the breed is.'

'I just thought – all them wrinkles.' Shelley's never seen a dog as ugly as this one. Why the fuck would anyone want a dog that bloody ugly? 'What's his name?' Shelley says.

'Beckett.'

'Did you call him Beckett for a reason?'

'Yes – I love Beckett.'

'If you love him so much why did you give him such a weird name?'

'Do you know who Beckett is?' Geraldine asks, slowly and pointedly.

'Yes,' Shelley replies, slowly and pointedly. 'He's your dog.'

Jesus, Shelley thinks, how thick is this woman?

Geraldine gives up trying to explain and returns to her agenda. 'Now, a few questions,' she continues efficiently.

'OK. You wanna sit down?' Shelley offers politely. Better be nice to her – there might be more cash where that last lot came from and Marlon's desperate for a new refracting telescope.

'Er no, thanks,' says Geraldine, remembering the absence of the cloth. 'You go ahead though.' As she watches Shelley squeeze her thighs under the kitchen table Geraldine can hardly believe her luck. She's really struck gold – this woman is a genuine freak.

Shelley sits down and rips open a bumper size pack of salt'n'vinegar crisps. 'OK with you if I eat while we talk?'

'No, no, good idea, you go ahead, keep your strength up. Now this is the deal. We film you here, now, then this evening you come to the theatre up in the West End where you and Serena will be on stage and on TV at the same time in front of a live audience. Then I'll ask you lots of easy questions about Serena like – what does she have for breakfast or. . .'

'But I dunno what she has for breakfast.'

'No, but then I'll say something like – oh, I believe it's scrambled eggs, isn't it? Or I'll say, what's her favourite colour? Is it true it's purple and you'll just say, yes, it is purple. OK?'

'OK,' Shelley mutters. She's trying to concentrate but it's hard because she's got something warm and wet going high up between her legs – it's this woman's bloody dog which is thrusting his soggy nose into her crotch. 'But what if other fans like me what know her mum's really called Barbara and lives in Gerrards Cross and collects jelly moulds see me on the telly and say I'm not real?' says Shelley, trying to break the dog's neck under the table without Geraldine noticing.

'That's not a problem. Once you're on the television you're more real than reality, don't worry about that. You just let me take care of things, I know what I'm doing. So we need to find out a little more about you. Do you, for example, have a job?'

'Yeh. I'm a writer,' says Shelley.

'Are you really?' gasps Geraldine. 'So what is it you write – poetry, novels, plays? Goodness, it might be something I know!'

'Well, it's hard to say . . .' Shelley begins.

'Oh, I see – you mean your letters. You write your begging letters.'

'Yeh. I write them. But that's not what I really like to write. What I really write is cards.'

'Cards?'

'Yes. Greetings cards. The poems, you know, what are in them. Cards for special occasions. Like when you retire, marry, lose a pet. I get paid but it ain't much. I'm doing a big series on the end of relationships at the moment because there's a lot of that about nowadays. Took me all morning to think of something what rhymed with loss.'

Geraldine stares. 'And what did you think of?'

'Albatross,' Shelley replies proudly.

Nothing is said for a while. The dog is noisily licking the space between Shelley's thighs – dogs always go for the strong smell trapped between the folds of her flesh there – and seems impervious to the fact that she's twisting one of his ears so hard it's about to fall off.

'Sorry but why are you telling me all this? What good is writing greetings cards for a TV show? No one's going to give a toss about that. Greetings cards aren't of interest to anyone. What we want is deviation, dysfunction, fetish – anything like that?'

Shelley looks at her nervously. 'Well, sometimes when I'm in a bit of a mood I go down to Somerfield in my leggings without any knickers on underneath,' she suggests helpfully.

Geraldine purses her lips. 'OK, let's just stick to the important stuff, shall we? Now my crew will film the flat, you don't mind if they go through your wardrobes and drawers do you? It's just a way of getting to know you better, and then –'

Suddenly Geraldine is interrupted by three violent thuds from the room next door, as if someone is banging on the floor with a stick.

'My God!' Geraldine jumps and yells. 'What was that?'

Shelley listens intently. 'That were three, weren't it?' she says.

'Yes. Yes, three. What on earth is it?'

'It's Marlon. My son.'

'What's he doing?'

'Banging on the floor with a stick.'

'Is he – strange?'

'No. He's hungry. One bang is when he wants a cup of tea. Two bangs is a cup of tea and cheese on toast – just a snack. Three bangs – he wants his dinner.'

'How old is your son?'

'Twenty-six.'

'Twenty-six? Why doesn't he get the food for himself?'

'Why should he when he's got his mum here to do it for him?' she retorts with pride.

Shelley gets up and starts busying herself with the grill and pulling boxes out of the freezer which is thick with ice that has been variously stained red and grey.

Geraldine knows, from the plays of Bertolt Brecht, that mothers are very attached to their sons so she tries to think of something to ask about Shelley's. 'What kind of work does he do, your son?' she asks.

'He's an astronomer.'

'Is he? My goodness. How fascinating. Where did he train?'

'In the lounge.'

'In the lounge?'

'Yes. He's very clever.' Shelley's face lights up. 'He's my pride and joy. He's a genius.'

'All mothers think that,' Geraldine remarks indifferently.

'No. He's a real genius. Mathematics. You know, numbers. He's a maths genius, even though he never went to school.'

'He never went to school?'

'Nope.'

'Did Marlon not go to school because he has ... a problem?'

'Oh no! No! No problem at all. It's just I wanted him at home with me really. Wanted to look after him, take care of him. Schools can be a hit and miss, can't they? Teachers what aren't getting enough and take it out on the kids and other kids what bully you. I reckoned he'd be better off at home watching the telly. He learnt everything he needed to know from that. TV is ever so educational, you know, if you just pick the right programmes. I made him watch all the documentaries, the quiz shows, games shows about what's the capital of Peru and all that stuff. You can learn ever such a lot that way.'

'What about friends? Girlfriends?'

'Nah. He don't need them, he's got me, hasn't he? We've always looked after each other. We've not needed no one else. We used to have so much fun when he was little. We watched TV together then. Especially the sci-fi. We'd sit up late together watching all them creepy sci-fi movies, right from when he was a baby he liked watching those. We both loved them films. No harm in that, is there? Just a bit of entertainment.'

'Of course,' Geraldine agrees politely.

'Yeh,' Shelley continues wistfully, 'He can't do words, you know, reading, writing. We never got round to that. He can only do numbers but he can do them brilliant. Especially them prime ones. He says it's the prime numbers what hold the secret to the universe. He did tell me what prime numbers are, but I forgot. Summat to do with a number what goes into a number. He was OK till he was about 16, yeh, about 16, then he started saying he felt like the numbers was starting to get too big in his head. He said he felt like his head was going to explode. That's when he went different.'

'Different?'

'Yeh, that's when it started, well, with the aliens. He said he was going to be able to communicate with them, through the numbers. I shouldn't tell you this but – what he's been doing is looking out for signs of an alien invasion. He's got this theory you see, that the aliens want to take over the earth and he thinks if he can find them and stop them then the whole human race will be saved.'

Geraldine is enthralled. Geraldine couldn't have invented this woman if she'd tried.

'And you, you believe this do you?'

Shelley thinks of the brooch and wrings her large hands.

'I might do.'

'OK. Good. That's good.' Nuts, nuts, nuts, Geraldine concludes gleefully. This is her first experience of genuine insanity. Of course there is a lot of madness in theatrical circles but most of it purely for effect. This is the kind of bonkers that will send the ratings into orbit.

'I know it sounds weird –'

'– no! No, it sounds fine!'

'– but the thing is he thinks he's worked out they're on their way. Don't ask me how – he can't do words and I can't do numbers. But I can't say to him don't worry, love, it'll never happen because it might, mightn't it? It might, they might invade and then how would I look? Dead. That's how I'd look. Dead and stupid. The thing is – he might be right. You think just because he's some kid on a council estate in Brentford what's never been to school it's all bollocks. But what if he really is a maths phenomenon what's discovered, through prime numbers, the secret to the universe? Look at Baby Jesus. Look what they thought about him.'

'Right,' agrees Geraldine piously.

'Anyway,' Shelley sniffs, 'it don't matter what other people think. All he cares about is his mathematics and his studies of the stars and the aliens what he thinks are going to invade the earth any minute.'

'You mean the aliens who are going to invade the earth.'

'Yeah, that's what I just said.'

'No, you always say what when you mean who.'

'When do I say what when I mean who?'

'Well, just then, for example, when you talked about the aliens.'

'When I talked about the aliens I said what?'

'Yes. You said the aliens "what". You should say "who" when referring to people.'

'You think aliens are real people?'

'Well, yes, yes, from a grammatical perspective they are people, aren't they?'

'So – you believe in aliens just like what my Marlon does?' Shelley gasps. Fuck. She's always thought all this alien talk was a bit crazy but now even this woman's saying she believes him. Maybe she should never have doubted her Marlon. Maybe what he's saying really has been real all along!

'So they're going to invade the earth soon are they?' Geraldine asks enthusiastically.

'No.'

'No? Oh, dear,' Geraldine's heart sinks.

'No. It's worse than that,' Shelley whispers conspiratorially. 'They're already here. They've already landed. And Marlon, he's met one of them.'

'Marlon has met an alien?'

'Yes. And she's –'

'– yes?'

'Serena Dawlish!'

'Serena Dawlish is an alien?' Oh thank you Lord, thank you, thank you, Geraldine thinks to herself, this just keeps on getting better. 'I think you should say that on the show. If you believe it, as you say you do, I think it's your duty, to reveal that on the show.'

Shelley's eyes grow wide and her mouth hangs open. 'So when I'm on the show I can say all this? I can say whatever I like?'

'Of course, my dear! No holds barred! You go for it.'

Meanwhile Geraldine's one step ahead. If the mum is barmy it sounds like the son is even barmier. 'What about Marlon? Can we include him on the show in some way? Get him to explain how he knows that Serena's an alien.'

'Oh no, I don't think so!' Shelley cries appalled. She can't get her baby boy involved in this show. If he saw Serena Dawlish again, it might finish him off completely.

'I'd double the money.'

Shelley hesitates. She thinks of that refracting telescope. 'Well, I dunno, I'm not sure . . .' she mumbles.

What's the big deal about the son? Geraldine wonders. Why does Shelley want to exclude him? Maybe he's got two heads or something. Either way, it's Geraldine's duty as an investigative television producer to find out. Her instinct tells her there's a story here, a story of human tragedy and pain, and it's her responsibility to unravel it and present it on primetime TV. She's just wondering what excuse she can give to go and suss Marlon out when Shelley finally loses patience with Geraldine's dog nuzzling her private parts and treads quietly but firmly on its paw. Beckett squeals, Geraldine squeals and picks him up.

'Oh dear,' says Shelley innocently, 'what's wrong with him?'

'He needs to go wee-wee. Can I use your loo?'

'For the dog?'

'Yes. He won't go wee-wee outside where people can see.

He's sensitive and very highly strung. It's the pedigree. I hold him over the bowl. Don't worry, he's more accurate than a human.'

The dog continues to howl and whimper. 'I think it's urgent. If I don't take him now his little bladder will give way and he might do it here on your kitchen floor!' she cries.

'OK, OK,' Shelley says although her kitchen floor has seen much worse. She heaves herself up from the table and takes Geraldine through to the bathroom. Geraldine hangs her pet over the toilet bowl. 'Would you mind shutting the door?' she says. 'He's very shy.' Shelley grunts her disapproval, closes the door and shuffles back to her crisps.

Geraldine leaves Beckett in the bath tub and creeps out of the bathroom to the tiny coffin-shaped hall. She turns left, in the direction where the banging noise came from. The door of the room is lightly ajar. She peeks through the crack into the room.

A man is in there, in an armchair; all she can see is the top of the back of his head. She can hear that he is sobbing. He is leaning forward cradling his head in his hands. Her heart is pounding. Will it be The Elephant Man? Suddenly Beckett, who has somehow managed to clamber out of the bath, comes strutting past her and walks straight up to Marlon. Marlon swivels round and sees Geraldine crouching in the doorway.

Geraldine gasps and freezes, terrified but more than that, astonished.

Marlon is not elephant. Marlon is handsome. And not just handsome – he is simply the most attractive man she has ever seen. A shaft of blond hair, thick and unkempt but lustrous, falls low over his face. He has a strong, pleasing jaw, and soft, large, even green eyes. His body is tall and athletic, his muscles visible through the fabric of his T-shirt. He looks like a statue in the Piazza Signoria.

He glares at her. 'Don't think I don't know who you are.'

'Oh!' she replies, flattered, wondering when someone like him would have ever gone to the theatre. 'Which of my productions did you see?'

'I know who you are. You and your dog. They have sent you to spy on me.'

So – it is as Geraldine thought. He is as weird as his mother. Fab. Two for the price of one. 'Well, actually, I'm Geraldine Fortescue, the producer of a television show which is going out live this evening and I was wondering whether you'd like to take part,' she says pleasantly.

'You can give me whatever story you like. I know that the data you provide them with will help them plan how they are going to use me for their experiments and, unless I can stop them, terminate me. And if I fail to stop them that is the end – for everyone. So if I perish, if my mother and the entire human race is wiped out, it will be because of you.'

'OK,' says Geraldine. 'I'll bear that in mind. And how do you know all this exactly?'

'I've seen the sign.'

'Right,' says Geraldine slowly.

The trouble is, he doesn't look mad. He looks quite totally, unbearably desirable. Of course it is absurd for a woman like Geraldine even to consider romance with a man like Marlon. She is almost 20 years older than him; he lives in a council flat; he does not have an Oxbridge degree closely followed by a distinguished career in the arts; he is nuts. He should, therefore, by all normal criteria, be automatically disregarded. The problem is that however many good reasons there are not to consider it, considering it is all she suddenly seems capable of. She forces herself to focus on the task in hand.

'The show is called "I Gave Birth To A Celebrity" starring Serena Dawlish.'

Marlon flinches. Serena Dawlish. Of course, that makes sense, Marlon thinks.

Marlon says, 'You know she's really an alien, don't you?'

'Yes,' Geraldine confirms gravely. 'Your mother was just telling me all about it. It's, well, it's come as rather a shock to me I must admit.'

'Yes. I met her. Yesterday. At a reading and writing class. She is an alien. I've the mathematical formulae to prove it.'

'Super. A bit of science never goes amiss. And are you prepared to come on the show and say all this to the audience, in front of Serena?'

'Of course!' Marlon cries. He knows this is something he must do. It is his duty to warn the world of Serena's presence amongst them, even though, at the very thought of seeing her again, a warm frisson of desire runs down the length of his spine.

Geraldine starts to get a bit nervous. This is getting very nutty. Should she let this man loose on her show? Shelley saying Serena's an alien is one thing. Shelley is overweight and unattractive and no one will take any notice of what she says. But if this man who is young and good-looking also says it and supports his arguments scientifically – well, that really would ruin Serena's reputation forever. No one would ever quite look at her in the same way. Her promotional earning potential would go up in smoke. It's one thing ending Serena's marriage but ruining her career as well? If Serena loses her part in 'Coombe Ridge Crescent' because people think she's extraterrestrial James' career will also suffer. Apparently the ads for his new production of 'Lear' have him billed as: 'James Marlborough – winner of six Oliviers and two Tonys and HUSBAND OF SERENA DAWLISH, STAR OF "COOMBE RIDGE CRESCENT" '. Geraldine had never planned to take things quite this far but that's the thing about professional hard-hitting investigative telejournalism – you never know where it's going to lead.

Can she really do this to James?

She tells Marlon she needs the loo where she smokes a ciggy to clear her head and checks through her mobile messages. That's when she hears the one from James telling her he can't hold her back in life and he's leaving her.

The bastard. He's changed his mind. Who the fuck does he think he is playing her like this? First he lied to her about his sex life and then he lied about leaving his wife. She is Geraldine Fortescue. He has toyed with the wrong woman this time. She will decimate him, annihilate him! She will use her show to get Shelley and Marlon to say Serena is an alien. Not only will the ratings go through the roof but James' and Serena's marriage and their careers will be over forever. There will be nothing left of James by the time she is done with him!

She returns to the sitting room. 'So, Marlon,' she announces grandly, 'this is all wonderful. You are going to come on the show this evening and tell the world that Serena Dawlish is an alien and you're going to prove it mathematically, is that correct?'

'Yes,' says Marlon fervently, 'yes, I am. Do you think that people will believe me?'

'Once it's on TV people will believe anything, my dear. Don't you worry. You're doing the right thing, you really are. Now, is there anything you wanted to ask me before you go on the show?'

He looks at Geraldine. Why is she being so nice? Can he trust her or not? It's obvious she's not an alien. It stands to reason that if you were an extraterrestrial who was going to take all the time and trouble to morph yourself into human form, you wouldn't bother to do it only to become a middle-aged woman who's too thin, with a lined, droopy face, a big nose and a flat chest. You'd want to look like Serena – oh God, Serena – someone totally gorgeous. Maybe this one was human but they've already abducted her, done their experiments on her and turned her into some kind of human spy for them.

Geraldine can see him staring at her, examining her with a fierce intensity. She considers his furtive glances and she understands. She must be a source of total fascination to him. An educated, sophisticated woman of the kind he has never known before. Geraldine is naturally intuitive about these things – being a theatre director she is a people person after all. It is clear he has fallen in love with her. She realises that if she is going to get him on the show she must move carefully – handle the situation with grace and sensitivity. No doubt he is suppressing countless fantasies about her. She must gently but firmly help him to see the impossibility of his dreams. She cannot encourage him. She cannot. He is vulnerable and naive. She is a cultured woman in her prime. She would overwhelm him. Disorientate him.

She decides to be open with him.

'I know what you think about me, Marlon,' she says. 'I know that my being here has caused you some – what shall we say – difficulty. I know that when you look at me you feel confused, questioning.'

Marlon gasps. It is as if she can read his mind (maybe, after what they've done to her, she can?). At least she is being honest. 'Yes, you're right,' he stammers.

'You feel, shall we say, that you want to get to know me . . . better?'

'Yes.'

Geraldine must tread so carefully. She must remember that this is a man who has not read Austen, Wordsworth or Hardy. He will not be capable of nuance, of subtlety, of litotes or satire. She must choose her words well. She must try and ignore the strange feelings of lust surging through her body at the sight of this man's biceps.

'OK, OK, that's good, good that we can be frank with each other. It must be hard for you to have to talk to me, a woman like me.'

'Yes. It is. Very hard. Because I don't know if I can trust myself with you.'

Trust himself to resist her is what he means. Geraldine

understands that. 'OK. Well why don't you ask me questions, anything you like. See if that helps.'

'Any question I like?'

'Sure.'

'OK.' He decides to put her to the test on what the alien was saying to him. 'I'm thinking about sex.'

So, surmises Geraldine, it is as I thought. He is infatuated with me.

'I see,' she sighs.

'Yes,' he says. 'What is sex?'

'Sex?'

'Yes. What is it?'

'You don't know what sex is?'

'Well, I'm not very clear on the detail of what you need to do . . .'

It is all so obvious. He wants her to teach him, show him, guide him . . . The older, experienced woman, every young man's fantasy.

'Which bit are you not sure about, exactly?' she says moving closer to him on the sofa.

'All of it.'

'You mean – no one's ever told you anything?'

'No.'

She can hardly believe it. 'So you want me to show you, to teach you, how to have sex?'

'Eurgh no,' he says. He doesn't want this old crow showing him anything. It would put him off his dinner. 'Just tell me.'

God, he's so shy.

'Well,' she begins. 'In a way it's simple and in a way it's not.'

'Give me the simple way,' he urges her.

'Um, well the simple way is that when a man and a woman sleep together they –'

'– you do it in your sleep?'

'No, that's just an expression for sex, like making love.

What happens is the man has a penis — yes, that — and the man puts it inside a woman here.'

Marlon's jaw drops. 'No!' he gasps, horrified. 'You're having me on. He puts this actually inside the woman?'

'Yes.'

'My God. How disgusting. I think I'm going to be sick.'

Geraldine swallows hard. So — how can he be having lustful thoughts about her if he doesn't even know what lust is?

'And then, when he's done that?' Marlon asks, horrified.

'Well, then he keeps sort of pushing it in and out —'

'You're not making this up are you?'

'No! No, I mean, everyone knows, well, people do generally know about it, it's just that you've never . . . Anyway, yes, he pushes it in and out and, well, it feels very nice.'

So that's it, Marlon thinks. That's what Serena, the alien woman is up to. She has found out that humans do sex and that they like it and she has deliberately made herself really attractive so that Marlon will want to sex with her. Fine. She may be smart but he's smarter. He'll let her think he's going to do it and then at the last minute, he won't and by then he'll have all her secrets and he'll be the one in charge. So he needs to find out more. He needs to know exactly how it's done so he can get his strategy right.

'So how does the man get it in her?'

'Well, when he has an erection, when it gets hard, he just pushes it in.'

Suddenly many things become clear to Marlon. This explains so much. This explains why, in the evening and then in the morning, and quite a few times during the day as well, he's been so stiff. Because he wants to do the sex thing! He had always thought there was something wrong with it! There isn't! He's normal! He clutches at Serena's brooch which he has been turning over and over in his hand ever since she gave it to him and suddenly feels a stab of hope.

'So can any man do this . . . thing with any woman. Like, could I do it with you?'

Geraldine feels the blood rush to her cheeks. What has she done? What has she unlocked here? He is her responsibility now. It is she who has awakened him and now this strange creature, this gullible, disorientated, infatuated, well-hung manboy, is brimming over with passion for her.

'Yes. In theory. Although obviously you should only do it with a woman for whom you have very strong feelings of desire, a woman you look at and find physically very attractive,' she says, feeding him his lines. She wishes he would stop fiddling with whatever it is he's holding in his hands while she's talking to him, she can't abide fidgets.

'Mmm,' Marlon computes. That's why he gets no reaction at all to this old woman. And who would? He wonders about the old, unattractive ones like her, what do they do? Does anyone ever bother with women like her? Do they just accept no one is going to want to sex with them and just give up all hope?

'I suppose you're imagining what it would be like with me?'

'Yes,' he says. Horrible, he thinks.

'Look,' says Geraldine patiently, earnestly, 'there's no point chasing an impossible dream. No point in pining for what you can't have.'

She's right, of course. The alien woman doesn't really care about him. All she wants is to get him in her specimen jar. 'No. I know that,' he agrees miserably.

Steady on, thinks Geraldine, no need to give up that easily!

'On the other hand, sometimes if we pursue the object of our affection with enough effort and energy you never know what might happen . . .'

'Do you really think so?' Marlon asks hopefully, looking up.

'Possibly,' Geraldine replies enigmatically, 'except would you mind, while we're discussing this, not playing with that thing in your hands all the time, it's really getting on my nerves?'

'It's not a thing!' Marlon cries, holding up the brooch. 'It's the alien's sign! She gave it to me! It's the mathematical formula that explains prime numbers! It's the sign I saw on the broken TV screen! It's the sign that she's an alien!'

'What? That? Don't be ridiculous. That's the Xerxes Carmen logo,' sniffs Geraldine looking at it. It must be a cheap copy of the coveted XC insignia which his mother has bought from some market stall – the real thing is made of white gold and is worth thousands.

'Xerxes Carmen?'

'Yes. He's a fashion designer. Serena is representing him this season, it was in all the papers. She has to wear his clothes all the time. This is his logo – the initials intertwined.'

'So this is just like – a fashion brooch?' he asks incredulously.

'Er, yes. Anyway, where were we? Ah yes, the pursuit of desire,' she murmurs, parting her legs suggestively. 'Perhaps you should think less about the stars and more about what's here, on Earth, right in front of you.'

Marlon's brain races. So – if this is just a fashion logo and not an extraterrestrial astrological mathematical sign then Serena isn't an alien.

And if Serena isn't an alien then – she's real.

And if she's real maybe there are – no aliens.

And if there are no aliens there will be – no invasion.

And if there is no invasion – he doesn't have to stay in this fuck-awful flat all day working out prime numbers, looking up telescopes and eating his mother's soggy cheese on toast.

Marlon feels the planet spinning under his feet. Oh God, all the time he's wasted when he could have been out there sexing with women like Serena! And now he can, now he can! This old woman's right, she's right! He doesn't want to look at bloody stars any more! What he wants to do now, more than anything, more than breathe, is to do the have sex make love sleep with thing with Serena! More than wants – he's desperate, desperate, desperate for her! He holds his fist tight to his mouth as if he is about to explode. He thinks of Serena, of her moist full lips and her long warm legs and all he's got here is this dry old stick woman! He cannot bear it!

'You're right!' he gasps.

Geraldine was worried she might be. She nods sympathetically. Oh dear, what have I done? she wonders enthusiastically. I've come into this house and totally overwhelmed this poor boy. What's he going to do now? she speculates in a state of excited horror. His breathing is fast and shallow. His eyes are wild. Geraldine grasps the seat of her chair. Maybe he's going to jump on her, force himself upon her! One flicker of encouragement on her part, Geraldine calculates, and he'll be on top of her, pushing her down on the sofa, his young, strong body making passionate love to her. She makes herself think of her TV show, her ratings. It would be so easy to let this young man take her, but she needs to keep him focused on the show, on Serena. She must see sense, exercise restraint and keep a level head. Success before love, always remember that. Sense not feeling. Brain not heart. Ratings not romance.

She stands and says, 'I must go now. Can I count on you to come on the show tonight with Serena?'

Marlon nods wordlessly and she leaves the room. One moment longer and their limbs would have been entwined, she knows that. He would no longer have been able to resist. She sighs. There was so much she would have been able to teach him, there on his mother's sofa in the lounge, so much he will now never know.

*

When Geraldine goes back to the kitchen Shelley has disappeared. The camera crew still standing waiting despondently in the kitchen inform her that Shelley has gone to the pub which is apparently what she always does at this time to watch the 2 o'clock episode of 'Coombe Ridge Crescent' on the big screen there.

Perfect, thinks Geraldine. First we show the film of the revolting flat, then we show an empty, grimy kitchen, then we film Shelley, mother of Serena, whom we have found swilling down lagers – or whatever it is that common people drink – in the pub.

She picks up Beckett and commandeers her troupe of men to follow her down the streets behind the Half Acre into the pub where she finds Shelley gazing at Serena on the screen.

Serena is lying on a couch; she is dressed in a long purple silk evening gown with diamond chandelier earrings spilling from her lobes, sipping from a glass of champagne. A man is sitting sobbing next to her.

'I love you, Sue, I always have and I always will.'

'I warned you, Bill,' Serena murmurs. 'I told you. If you didn't buy me that engagement ring – you would never have me back! And now – you never will!'

The man falls to his knees.

'I'm begging you, Susan, I'm begging you! Have pity on me!'

'I have no pity! Only hate! Now I am going to marry your brother and there's nothing, nothing you can do to stop me!'

Shelley is close to tears.

Geraldine sits down at the table next to her.

'Sorry I didn't stay but it was time for "Coombe Ridge Crescent".'

'Oh, don't worry about that. Listen,' says Geraldine, 'I've been thinking. I need a man.'

'Eh?'

'Yes. A man to be Serena's dad on the show,' says Geraldine earnestly. 'Do you have, I don't know, a boyfriend who would be happy to get involved?'

'Well, yes,' says Shelley coyly. 'There are various men in my life.'

'Great,' says Geraldine. 'Anyone I can ring?'

'Oh yeah, there are loads of blokes.'

'Right,' says Geraldine cheerfully. Then, after a pause, 'Well – like who, for example?'

'Well, I dunno, um,' Shelley stammers, 'There's him, for example,' she says gesturing towards a man at the bar.

'Him?' says Geraldine, taking in the scruffy, sweaty, middle-aged creature. His face looks like it has been carved from a turnip with a hacksaw; he is bald apart from a greasy grey pony tail gathered from those few wisps of hair still clinging stoically to the back of his shiny head. 'He's one of your boyfriends?'

'Well, not exactly my boyfriend but, you know, I'm single and so's he, well not exactly single but his wife's not into it any more so often we . . . you know, now and then, when he's got nothing better to do and I haven't either we, well, we meet up.'

'So he's just someone you fancy?'

'Nah, I don't fancy him. I don't even like him. He's just handy for a shag.'

'But how can you allow yourself to be . . . penetrated by someone you don't even like?'

'Penetration?' Shelley exclaims through her full open mouth. 'Nah. There's no penetration. Only oral.'

Geraldine looks at him and imagines what his genitals must taste like. She feels the quails eggs she had for breakfast curdle in her stomach.

'What you making that face for?' Shelley complains.

'I'm just wondering – is that pleasant for you?'

'Pleasant? Not really. But then, when it's my turn, it makes it all worthwhile.'

'Your turn?'

'Natch!'

'You mean he – you –'

Shelley nods enthusiastically.

Geraldine looks at Shelley sitting on the wooden pub chair, at her splayed thighs stuffed into their shiny green leggings. As well as feeling mildly ill, she's wondering, given Shelley's size, how it's anatomically possible for a man to get his face in there anyway.

'Yes, he loves it, that one does,' Shelley continues energetically, seeing Geraldine's reaction. 'Loves it. He wants to be in there all the time. His cave he calls it. He's the cave man and he goes in his cave. Ugga, ugga, ugga, he goes. Ugga, ugga, ugga.'

'And you like it?'

'It's all right. Well, yes, I do. Although sometimes he goes on a bit. I'm done and he's still on with the ugga.'

Geraldine looks back at the man at the bar. She imagines him locked between Shelley's thighs going ugga. She wants to ask how he can go ugga if his mouth is full of . . . Shelley, but she's scared she might not be able to cope with the answer.

'So, I'll go and ask him if he wants to be on the show, shall I?' Geraldine says in desperation.

'If you like,' Shelley squirms.

'You don't look too keen on the idea.'

'Well, you know, he might not want to, seeing how, you know, he's married and all.'

'Don't worry, I'll offer him money.'

Shelley gives her a blank look.

Geraldine gets up, goes over and says, 'Look, I'm a TV producer and I was talking to your friend over there and –'

'What friend?'

'That woman, over there,' Geraldine points.

'That fat thing? She ain't no friend of mine.'

'Yes, don't worry, I know the situation is sensitive but I have money and I was wondering –'

'I've told you,' the man cries aggressively, causing globules of spittle to land in Geraldine's face, 'I don't know her, I've never spoken to her and you can shove your money!'

Geraldine takes a step back.

'So the word "ugga" means nothing to you?' she concludes pleasantly.

He glowers and looks for a moment as if he is about to hit her. Geraldine walks quickly away back to Shelley. She sits down at the table. 'That story about you and him, you invented all of that, didn't you?'

'Maybe,' Shelley mumbles.

'Oh for God's sake will you stop wasting my time and get real! This is television, this is serious! You can't go round all the time making things up! Please! Now, I've asked you to help me find someone who can be Serena's father for the show, a man with a bit of wow factor. What about Marlon's father? What happened to him, can we use him? Does he still see Marlon?'

'Nah. He's never seen him. He never knew my Marlon even exists.'

'Really? How fascinating. I wonder how different your life would have been if he had known – if he had stayed with you, married you, been a father to Marlon.'

'What's the fucking point of wondering that?'

'I'm a dramatist. Someone like me is accustomed to seeing life from different perspectives, envisaging alternative outcomes. Imagine it, Shelley,' Geraldine elaborates melodiously, 'imagine the scene where after twenty-six years he discovers that he has a son, now a grown man. Think of the passion, the excitement, the joy of the moment at which father and son are finally reunited. Imagine the ratings!'

'Yeah, except this is my life, not one of your bloody TV shows.'

'You might be able to track him down, rekindle your romance!' Geraldine speculates enthusiastically.

'Nah, that's never gonna happen. He'd never want me.'

Geraldine tries to think of something nice to say but the fact is that unless the gentleman concerned also had a body with the dimensions of a transit van there is indeed very little chance of this being the case. She decides to give up on the father of Marlon angle. It was probably unnecessary anyway – she already has the show of the century lined up for that evening. Serena Dawlish, superstar, complete with terminally embarrassing mother ready to say anything for a bit of cash and fit but peculiar brother happy to demonstrate mathematically that Serena is really an alien.

What more could any TV presenter want?

CHAPTER 9

It's show time.

Serena is in the car on the way to the theatre in Shaftesbury Avenue. She's so unhappy. She's missing Marlon. What is this love thing that you can't control it?

This whole show is worrying her. Serena has never even seen the presenter, some woman called Geraldine Fortescue, or the woman who's going to be her new mum. She asked Gareth about that, said maybe she should at least meet them before the show but apparently this Fortescue woman thought it would be more spontaneous if they met for the first time on stage. Serena thought this was a bit weird but Gareth said he was fine with it so she left it. Just then she gets a text from Gareth on her mobile telling her he's arranged for Alex Cordell to be in the audience so that half way through the show he can suddenly appear out of nowhere and declare his love for her. Gareth has been discussing things with Alex's manager and they've decided to drop the low key approach and go for a stronger, high profile strategy. Serena's past caring. If she can't have Marlon they can do what they like. She applies an extra layer of mascara, that always steadies her nerves, and looks out of the window at London flashing by. Chiswick, Hammersmith, Kensington, Knightsbridge, Piccadilly. Life feels a bit weird this evening; she feels a bit weird this evening. Everything was so much easier when all she had to worry about was handbags. Everything was so much easier when she wasn't in love.

★

Shelley and Marlon are in a taxi. She's never been in a taxi before but Geraldine sent them a taxi to take them to the theatre even though Shelley said the bus would do just as well and could she have the cash instead. Geraldine said no and that the taxi was on account and when Shelley asked what that meant she said it meant that Geraldine's production company would pay for the cab but how could they say they would do that even before they knew how much the cab was going to be? All the way there Shelley is tense and stressing about this, especially when she sees the meter on the black cab going up past the £20 mark – she's got £8.58 in her purse, she's just taken it out and counted it. What's she going to do if the cab driver says something like Geraldine only agreed to pay something like £10 on this 'on account' business and she has to make up the rest? There's going to be an awful scene and Marlon will get upset.

*

Marlon is with his mother in a cab on the way to the theatre. He is happy – he is going to see Serena and do the sex thing with her, now that he knows what it is. He's going to do it there and then, on the stage. Nothing will stop him now – he's been waiting all his life for this. Geraldine has explained to him he won't be meeting Serena straight away – he has to wait a bit then he'll be invited on stage and when that happens he can do what he likes. He should do what he likes. In fact, once he's on the stage, the more he shows his feelings the better, that's what Geraldine says. Marlon is so excited. His hands are sweating, his heart is beating and his willy is doing that stiff thing all the time now, all the time.

*

James is in the theatre bar on his fourth G&T. His agent has told him he's got to come here incognito this evening as a surprise guest for some show Serena's appearing in. He's always being yanked off to appear on endless bloody TV award ceremonies on his wife's behalf. There've been so many he's lost count and he's lost interest. His agent tells him it's good exposure for him. Normally James doesn't mind – there's usually plenty of free booze and plenty of young totty around but he's never been asked to go anywhere bloody incognito before. He told his agent that James Marlborough incognito is an oxymoron but she just went quiet so obviously the wretched woman calls herself a theatrical agent and doesn't even know what a bloody oxymoron is.

He's so fed up. He's already regretting his decision not to leave Serena. He'll just have to get cracking seducing that girl who's playing Cordelia – he never can remember her damn name – although someone has told him she's just got engaged to some young Hollywood drip so now he's going to put in a bit of effort to convince the wench to spread her legs.

He orders another drink and sits and waits for Serena's agent, that dreary Gareth with the shiny face and the clammy hands, to come and get him. He waits for someone in the bar to recognise him and ask for his autograph but when they see him they are so overwhelmed by him they are all too shy to come forward.

*

Barbara Dawlish is stuck in traffic on the M40 on the way to the theatre (for, sadly, Serena, what with all the emotional trauma of being newly in love, has forgotten to ring and let her know that her maternal services are no longer required).

Barbara has got her husband Roger to drive her down to London in their Nissan Micra. He's going to wait for her in the car while she goes in to the theatre and appears on the show. It's best that way. Roger isn't good with people and he'd only sit in the audience and fret about whether he'd remembered to lock the car.

This is the proudest moment of Barbara's life. Sometimes, in quiet moments down on her hands and knees with the begonias, she has wondered what the point of it all has been. Roger, troubled as he is by his on-going problem with premature ejaculation, has never been able to offer her a very full marriage and Serena was always such a wayward girl . . . Now, at last, it seems that it has all come good. Her daughter has become a famous actress and she, herself, is about to appear on national television. It has all been worthwhile after all. She has got everyone from the church watching this evening the proud moment when she will walk on stage in the West End and cry – Yes! I am mother to Serena Dawlish! I gave birth to this celebrity!

*

Christine Cazale has found out, through the soap grapevine, that she did not get the part of Bernice Overburton in 'Coombe Ridge Crescent' because Serena Dawlish told the producer that she suffers from cold sores. And she guessed from what Serena blurted out that she, Serena, must be the celebrity of the new TV show being filmed live that evening. Christine has rung Holly Diamond. Not only have they agreed that they are now going to be best friends but they have a plan; together they are going to the show to pull Serena's extensions out, live on national TV, with their own bare hands.

*

Geraldine Fortescue looks out from the wings at the packed theatre. It occurs to her that, really, she's about as good as it gets really. Double first in English from Corpus Christi, a glittering career in the theatre and now this. Only she could have pulled it off – not only to make the move from theatre to telly as she has, but to make it and make better telly than anyone else.

She has emailed everyone she knows to tell them to watch the show. The media are stacked up expectantly along the front row of the audience, cameras at the ready. The theatre is bursting at the seams and people who couldn't get a seat are standing in sub-zero temperatures on the pavement waiting to see the show on the big screens they have set up outside. Tomorrow Geraldine will be a household name. She will have every network in the universe in the country begging her to work with them. She takes one last look at the eager crowd before her then walks out onto the stage to meet her destiny and change everyone else's.

*

The lights dim.

Geraldine greets the audience, a throng of people who are here to see a celebrity, any celebrity, anyone famous will do. They will not be disappointed. They are, Geraldine announces, about to see a spectacle like no other. On this, the first in the new series of 'I Gave Birth To A Celebrity', they will, Geraldine confirms, witness the inner life of one of this country's most popular actresses, *the* most popular actress. As if on cue someone in the audience cries, 'Is it . . . Serena Dawlish?' – Geraldine need only nod and the crowd erupts. Yes, Geraldine confirms, tonight their celebrity is the amazing Serena Dawlish. They will understand her history, her personality, her pysche. Fuck that, the men think, as long as we get to see her tits, but the women appreciate the gesture and redouble the intensity of their applause. Geraldine goes to sit in a large purple velvet armchair. Next to her is a long, plush sofa where her guests will sit and, God willing, draw blood. Calmly, carefully, Geraldine rearranges the folds of her cerise alpaca kaftan. No one speaks, no one breathes.

'Before we start I'd like to introduce you to a man who is key in Serena's life – her manager, Gareth Sinclair.' Gareth appears on stage and sits on the sofa. 'Gareth,' Geraldine explains, 'is here in a legal capacity. Given her enormous fame, he must ensure he is happy with the promotional viability of her life as it is revealed.' The crowd grunt their approval. Fair enough, they think, someone of Serena's status warrants that although couldn't she have chosen someone who doesn't look quite so much like a toad?

'Hello, Geraldine,' Gareth says. 'Thank you for having me on your show. I hope you don't mind but I bumped into someone on the way down here and I've invited him to join us.'

Geraldine gives Gareth a polite look for have you gone quite mad?

'It's Serena's husband, James,' Gareth explains. He had rung James' agent earlier to tip her off about the show and told her to make sure James came to the theatre this evening. Then he could get him on stage and maximise the promotional impact of Alex Cordell's spontaneous outburst.

Initially Geraldine is infuriated by this but then she realises – it is an act of genius! She has been so used to thinking of their affair as clandestine but why not have him on stage and expose their relationship? Blow their marriage apart on her own show! How totally delicious. That will teach the man not to play with a woman like Geraldine Fortescue.

The audience murmurs with impatience and confusion. James Marlborough – who's he? Which soap is he on?

'But of course!' Geraldine cries. 'Ladies and gentlemen – James Marlborough, the actor!'

James is standing hovering in the wings. He's more than a little pissed on all that gin but you can hardly blame the bloke for over-indulging what with all that relational angst going on in his life. He hears his name called from the stage and for one horrible drunken moment he thinks he's heard Geraldine's voice. A nightmare scenario rushes through his head where he walks out on stage and there he is, under the full glare of the spotlight, on an awards show where it's his mistress who is presenting an award to his wife. He steadies himself and reminds himself he's had a bit to drink. 'Mr Marlborough – that's your call!' someone cries urgently from behind. He sallies forth, ready for the rapturous applause but the only time this lot have set foot in a theatre is for panto season. Aside from being Serena's husband, no one really has any idea who he is. A reluctant, hesitant ripple of clapping greets him.

James stops in his tracks but it is already too late. He is there, he has been seen.

Geraldine stands, glares at him with a slightly deranged

expression of triumph and says loudly, smugly, 'James, welcome to "I Gave Birth To A Celebrity"!'

OK, so his dream forecast wasn't quite accurate. This is not an awards show and his wife is not receiving an award which is not being presented by his mistress. No, this is a whole show dedicated entirely to his wife being produced as well as presented by his mistress, the mistress to whom he has just sent a text saying he wants to end their affair, the mistress who only the day before tried to kill herself in front of his own house. Somewhere through the haze of gin James is scared, really scared. He fears the worst, even though he knows that won't cover what a wrathful Geraldine is capable of.

'Please, take a seat,' Geraldine offers benignly, indicating a long sofa where Serena's agent is sitting grinning at him. He sits because he is too terrified to do anything else and hopes that if he sits quietly enough for long enough he'll wake up and the horrid dream will have all gone away. 'So we're going to start,' she announces finally, 'by seeing where Serena grew up – a deprived council estate in Brentford. Who would have thought that such glamour, such style could have been weaned in a place such as this. We think of Balzac, of Dostoevsky, of Stendhal. We think of O'Casey and O'Neill!'

Er, no we don't, darling. This language, these references – they're a tad too florid for the crowd she's got in-house. This ain't The National, and no one's quite sure what she's on about but they understand pictures and fortunately at this very moment that afternoon's filming appears on a vast screen at the back of the stage. We see a squalid council block, we see one of Geraldine's cameramen lying huddled on the ground in a state clearly intended to be that of a man high on an illegal narcotic substance, underneath a sign which reads 'NO BALL GAMES' with the word 'SHIT' scrawled roughly over it.

There is a gasp of shocked horror from the audience.

'Yes,' continues Geraldine's doleful commentary, 'this is indeed a desolate scene and yet the childhood reality for one of our best-loved actresses, what am I saying?, for our best-loved actress, Serena Dawlish.'

Repetition of the Serena Dawlish brand name goes down well and, in spite of their bewilderment, the audience breaks automatically into applause at the very mention of her name. The camera pans to the revolting stairwell, the walkway, the plastic flowers and the hideous yellow kitchen.

'We looked for Serena's mother but of course she was not here, she was not at home, she was where she has been for most of poor Serena's lonely youth – drinking down at the local pub.'

Geraldine allows a shiver of pleasure to shimmy down her spine. However well she might have hoped this would go, it's going better. The silence of the crowd, dumb with disbelief, their apprehension, their fear are almost overwhelming as they watch these ugly scenes, as they behold the indisputable evidence which topples their beloved icon down from the gilded pedestal on which they have so lovingly placed her.

The camera wings its way unerringly, unremittingly up the littered pavements of the back streets behind the Half Acre; it thrusts through the scarred doors of the pub into the grimy public lounge, it darts past the forlorn, beer-sodden tables, across battered, abandoned wooden chairs until it reaches a woman sitting alone surrounded by empty beer glasses stuffing large handfuls of crisps into her mouth, gazing at a vast television screen full of images of Sue Upton swanning around in silk and diamonds.

A fat woman.

An obesely fat woman.

Even before the words leave Geraldine's mouth the audience have guessed what she is about to say. Some of them clasp their hands to their ears, some turn away but in vain. They know, they know, they already know what can no longer be denied.

This is Serena Dawlish's mother.

And she is ugly. And she is fat.

As one they expel a groan of revulsion, a long eeuuuurgh of disgust.

'Yes!' cries Geraldine triumphantly. 'This is 'I Gave Birth To A Celebrity'! And this is Shelley – the woman who gave birth to Serena Dawlish!'

At this point loud trumpets break forth from some invisible orchestra and in wobbles Shelley, larger than life, fatter than ever, more vast even than the huge image of herself surrounded by empty glasses of Kronenberg on the screen stretched across the stage behind her.

'Shelley, welcome to the show,' Geraldine begins sincerely as she invites her to sit down. Shelley parks herself on the sofa alongside Gareth and James who make no bones about the discomfort they are experiencing being observed in public with someone who is not conventionally attractive.

'Tell us,' Geraldine continues earnestly, 'do you have any guilt for the childhood you put Serena through? Do you feel you have any apology you may want to make? Do you feel bad, now, about exploiting your poor daughter's name by coming on this show?' Shelley sits and stares at Geraldine blankly. Eh? This isn't what Geraldine said she was going to say. Nothing like it. So she says nothing and waits instead for her to tell her what to say like she said she would. But all Geraldine does is cock her head like a petulant budgie and sit and stare. The audience is starting to lose patience with this woman – first she's fat, second she's been a bad mother to their heroine, third she's got nothing to say for herself. She could be stupid so they could laugh at her; she could be stroppy so they could jeer at her; she could even be pathetic so they might feel a bit sorry for her. But just to sit there and be nothing! Well, it's not really on.

They start to boo and hiss, quietly at first but soon rising to a loud roar of displeasure.

'Fuck you!' says Shelley to Geraldine. Why is she not helping her out? When they hear this the audience only bray even louder.

'At this point,' Geraldine proclaims, standing and bidding them be calm with her hands, 'I think there is only one thing we can do – and that is get Serena on stage to ask her what she thinks!'

The audience falls at once to a hushed silence.

Serena.

Serena. What are they to think about Serena? Yes, she is their ideal, their icon, their idol but she has betrayed them. She is a goddess who, it turns out, is the progeny of something imperfect, something distinctly and indisputably unbeautiful. She has fat and ugly genes in her veins. She might at any moment cease to be immaculate and turn out to be as vulnerable as the rest of them – can they still trust her?

When Serena appears on stage the crowd is silent. Jesus, she really does exist. She really is a human being. And she looks more lovely, more desirable, more delectably symmetrical than ever. They want to applaud but their hands tremble separately in their laps. They love her and they want to be able to continue to love her – but can they? They want to see what she's going to do. They can hardly bear their own apprehension. Will she publicly acknowledge this maternal blubber?

'Welcome to "I Gave Birth To A Celebrity", Serena,' Geraldine chirrups.

Serena sees James. 'What's he doing here?' she asks.

'Who? Him? James Marlborough? Why, he's your husband, of course! He must be here to share your special moment. And you see we also have your manager, Gareth, and, last but not least, your mother!'

Serena takes one look at Shelley, turns to Geraldine and says, 'You've got to be bloody joking!'

Geraldine faces the audience. 'Of course there are tensions in a celebrity family just as there are in any other. There is history, there are complicated feelings at work, the result of years of suppressed emotions. I think I should warn you,' she says earnestly, 'that for reasons that will become understandable there is a lot of *anger* inside Serena, anger that has waited a long time to come out and will, I can assure you, be coming out here, live on stage this evening.'

'Are you doing this to get me back for leaving Marlon?' Serena hisses at Shelley.

Shelley looks terrified. She's about to cry, 'No, only for the money!' when Geraldine asks the audience to be patient, grabs Serena by the arm, switches off her mike and snarls in her ear, 'It's taken me weeks to plan this show and I'm not about to let you bugger it up! One more word and I'll let them all know that you're so desperate for success that you're even prepared to lie about the identity of your own mother!'

Geraldine switches the microphone back on. 'Sorry everyone but as you see, there's a huge amount of tension on stage as mother and daughter confront each other – almost as if for the first time. Perhaps, now the truth is finally out about Serena's past, it does indeed feel like the first time. Does it, Serena? Does it? Can you look at this woman and put your hand on your heart and accept that she is your mother?'

Serena is trapped. If she accepts this woman as her mother that's her glamorous image gone forever. If she disowns Shelley Geraldine will crucify her. Her fate teeters before her in all its existential glory.

Serena stands. She does not move. She does not speak. What should she do?

People sit forwards in their seats so they do not miss a word, a gesture.

'Hang on,' Serena says finally. She takes out her mobile phone and texts 'What now?' to Gareth who is sitting a few feet away from her. He texts her back, 'Get on with it!'

Exasperated Serena sits down next to Shelley. She says nothing but nothing is enough for Geraldine.

'Good. Right. At this point I would like you to tell us a bit about yourself, Shelley,' she continues. 'You had a tough time bringing Serena up as a single mother in Brentford, did you not? And is it not true that after Serena you had another child, a boy, Serena's brother, about whom she knows nothing?'

Serena's jaw drops. What is this woman on about?

'Yes, I do have a boy,' Shelley confirms proudly as a camera lurches expectantly into her face.

'In fact we have that son as a guest on our show today. Ladies and gentlemen – I present you Marlon!!'

At this Marlon wanders timidly onto the stage and there is a collective rush of blood to the heads of all the women.

Serena is appalled. 'He's not my brother!' she cries.

'You're in shock, in denial, Serena. Don't worry – it will pass,' Geraldine instructs firmly. 'Please, Marlon, sit down there, yes there, between your mother and your sister. Now Shelley, can you tell us about your relationship with their father?'

'Well,' stammers Shelley, 'they don't have the same dad . . . as far as I know.'

'As far as you know? I see. All a bit confusing for you, is it? Don't worry, take your time. The truth is sometimes hard to handle. Now tell us what do you know about Serena's father?'

'Only what I seen on her website, that he's a tool maker called Roger what lives in Gerrards Cross.'

'So – you're obviously not in contact with him?'

'Er, no.'

'And Marlon's father? Surely you can tell us more about him?'

Shelley feels her legs start to tremble and her forehead sweat. Her breathing becomes shallow and she has to grasp onto the sofa to keep her balance.

'Are you all right?' Geraldine asks nervously. Suddenly Shelley looks very pale, as if she might be about to faint or by-pass fainting and just crumple up and die. Although it does cross Geraldine's mind that having Serena Dawlish's mother die on the sofa would make great telly she needs to complete the full hour of the show or the advertisers will complain.

'The thing is,' Shelley stutters, as the most precious memory she has starts to seep back into her head, ' 'I've never told anyone the story of what happened between me and Jim,' she says. 'I've never told anyone, never.'

'That's OK. You take your time, it's just you, me and the nation listening,' Geraldine comforts her.

Shelley shuts her bulky eyelids and remembers.

*

It was 27 years ago but it might as well be 27 minutes because Shelley can still recall every detail of every moment of her watching him sitting there, with his friends, the other side of the pub. She's noticed him before. Of course she has. He's the handsome one. The cocky one. She's with her dad. Since her mum died last year she comes here with her dad. No sense in sitting home alone. She's 16. Fat. Very fat. Too fat to care much about it any more now. People say she was born fat. They say she'll die fat. Fat is what she is. Her skirt is tight. The hem of it makes a red mark on her thighs. A red line. Blue denim skirt, white thighs, red line. Her dad sits at the bar and smokes. He doesn't sit next to her at the pub. She sits at a table on her own until he tells her it's time to go. That's OK. She prefers it that way. The man, Jim, she's heard his friends call him that, is listening to one of them tell a joke. Shelley notices that the friend seems anxious, eager to please. She can see he wants to tell the joke well. He wants to make Jim laugh. He wants to impress him.

People think that because she's fat and they don't notice her that she doesn't notice them, but she does, she does.

The friend tells the joke. Jim laughs. But not sincerely. His laugh isn't really real. Shelley can see that. She wonders why Jim is laughing a not really real laugh. Is it to help the friend, make him feel OK? Or is it because Jim is false, only knows how to laugh a fake, forced laugh? Shelley wonders about that.

She moves her head to reach for her drink – a Pepsi, sipped slowly, it's got to last – and smells the smell of her life in her hair. The smell of the breakfast she cooked her dad that morning, the pet shop where she works as a cleaner after school, the sweat she broke into when she ran for the bus, the burgers she fried for her dad's tea.

She should wash her hair more often. Except it only gets dirty again. This is a thought she thinks often. So much of what she does she does all the time, again and again. Every day again. Washing, brushing, cleaning, wiping, cooking, pissing, shitting. Shelley reckons that most of what she does in any one day she does every day. Her life is almost always the same. Almost always.

Even her thoughts are the same. Whatever Shelley thinks every day, she's thought it before. Like – why the fuck did my mum have to die so soon? Why can't I have a different dad? Why can't my dad die immediately of a mysterious illness? Why am I so fat? Why do I live in Brentford when there's a whole world out there? Why do I work in a pet shop every evening after school when the smell makes me puke? Why am I me? She hardly ever has a new thought in her head. If she were to have a genuinely new thought in her head, she thinks, it would probably knock her out.

She's looking at Jim. One of his friends looks at her looking at him and nudges him and he looks at her. He smiles, the friend says something else, then Jim stops smiling. The friend nudges him again and whispers something else in his ear. The friend laughs. Jim doesn't laugh. Not even his fake laugh, he doesn't even laugh that. Then the friend says something to all the men round the table and they all laugh. Jim finishes his beer. Then he stands up. For a moment she thinks – as if! – he's going to walk over to her. But he heads for the gents. His friends laugh and cheer. He goes to the gents then after one minute, maybe two, he's out again. And he walks towards Shelley.

'Come outside,' he says.

'You what?'

'Come outside, with me,' he says.

Shelley gets up and goes. Shelley's always done what she's told.

When they get outside Jim puts her against the wall, lifts up her skirt, brings down her knickers, gets inside her, pushes a bit and pulls out. He wipes the rest of the wet off his spent prick with his hands, dries them on the sides of his jeans and does up flies. Then he stands next to her, against the wall, and lights a cigarette. He offers her a puff which she takes, not because she has ever smoked a cigarette before but because she wants her lips to go where his have been.

He says nothing. She says, 'What was it your mate said to you?'

'What?'

'Your mate, that one what's sitting in there next to you, what was it he whispered in your ear when you was looking at me?'

He shakes his head. 'You don't want to know.'

'I do. I've asked, haven't I? I do want to know, I've asked so I do, I fucking do want to know!'

'All right. He said – I'll bet you a fiver you wouldn't shag that fat slag.'

The words leave his mouth, fly across and pelt her, pinning her hard against the brick wall, so hard she can feel the brick scour the skin on her back through the cold nylon of her school shirt.

'I see,' she says, but only to make sure she can still speak, to ground herself, to check she's still alive and breathing. 'And then, he said something a second time. What did he say then?'

'The second time? The second time he said he'd make it a tenner if I could get you to say you loved me.'

Shelley closes her eyes. Her breathing stops. Her skin sweats. She parts her lips to speak and say something. She's not sure what that something's going to be till she hears it said. 'So . . .' she pushes the words out, 'What are you going to do now? Are you going to make me say I love you?'

He shakes his head. 'Nah,' he says. 'I'm not going to do that.'

She's watching him now. 'What are you going to do?'

'I'm going to do this.' He comes very close. His semen is running down between her thighs. He cups her cheeks in his palms. She feels the tips of his fingers warm at the corners of her eyes and the flesh of her full face spilling through between them. 'Uh,' she whispers. 'Uuh,' she groans. She can hardly bear to stand. He brings his lips close to hers and holds them there so she can smell the stale stink of tobacco and sour food on his breath. He kisses her. So light. So gentle. He whispers, 'I love you.' Then again, firmer, 'I love you.' He takes away his hands, takes away his fingers, takes away his body and goes slowly, back towards the pub.

Shelley is half-dead up against the wall. Her back is slipping down, her legs are buckling, her lids are collapsing in their sockets but she can see him moving through half-closed eyes.

'Where are you going?' she murmurs after him.

'Back inside,' he says airily, 'to get in a round with my winnings,' he laughs. When, later, she goes back in he's sitting at the table with his friends. He leaves half an hour after that. He does not say goodbye. She never sees him again.

'Nine months later I had my son, Marlon. But I never saw Jim again. Never. Not once.'

★

No one knows quite what to make of this. There's no story-line, no plot, just pain. What's the point of that? Marlon, especially, looks a little stunned as somewhere during the course of his 26 years his mother has omitted to tell him this story.

'So he has no idea that Marlon even exists?' Geraldine enquires gaily.

'We only met that once. I know nothing about him, what became of him, only that his name was Jim. And he never even knew I was pregnant.'

'Would you recognise him again if you were to see him again do you think?'

'Oh yeh!'

'How can you be so sure?'

'Cos he had a funny mark on him.'

'A funny mark? Where?' Geraldine insists.

'On his dick.'

At this the audience falls about in collective hysterics. She's not so bad after all, the fat lady. That story went on a bit, but she's making up for it now. Geraldine too is laughing. The sweet smell of success on this show is so pungent it's almost knocking her out.

'What sort of a funny mark?' Geraldine asks.

'I remember, you know, when he was cleaning it afterwards' – more howls of laughter from the audience – 'I saw it in the pub light. It was fishy.'

'Fishy?' Geraldine squeals, giving the audience time to gather themselves from their fits of mirth. 'How do you mean – fishy?'

'It was something about a carp. It was tattooed all the way up his privates.'

Suddenly Geraldine is not laughing.

Geraldine says, 'It was 'carpe diem'.'

'Yeh, yeh, that's it! How do you know that?'

'His name was Jim and he had 'carpe diem' tattooed on his penis,' Geraldine groans and looks at James.

Serena looks at James then back at Geraldine. She says to Geraldine, 'How do *you* know that?'

Geraldine sits back in her seat in disbelief. She's finding it difficult to keep up. She's doing her best here to create a wonderful show but the bloody truth keeps getting in the way.

'Well,' says Geraldine philosophically, 'I'm sure at this stage the person we'd all like to meet is this Jim, the Jim who seduced an innocent 16 year old at the back of a pub all those years ago and deserted her, the Jim who is the father of your son, Marlon, the boy you've had to bring up alone all these years.'

The audience all turn and stare at each other. So this Jim, the bastard, is already amongst them. This is getting good. Who can it be?

'How would you feel about that, Shelley?' Geraldine asks compassionately.

Shelley looks blank. 'What you on about? I told you, I ain't seen him for 27 years. I got no idea who he is now.'

'He is the man sitting next to you.'

'You what?' Shelley turns and stares at James. There's no mistaking the sudden rush of recognition which spreads over her face. Her lower lip starts to wobble. She cannot speak.

At this point James, who hasn't been paying that much attention to all this made-for-TV nonsense, starts to compute certain facts. First – there are only three men on stage. Second – one of them is Marlon, this horrendous woman's son and therefore an unlikely candidate for also being his own father; the other is Gareth, the queerest manager in the business and therefore unlikely to be father to anyone. Third – everyone is looking at him, James. Fourth, Jim is a derivative of his name James. Fifth – he did shag a lot of girls in his youth. This list could go on but stops when Geraldine gets up, stands behind him, puts a hand lightly on his shoulder and says, 'Is this the man, Shelley? Is this man, James Marlborough, this country's greatest stage actor, husband to this country's greatest TV actress, Serena Dawlish, is he the one?' she whispers because, by now, the auditorium is so awash with appalled silence that even her whisper rings out like a bellow.

Shelley nods.

'Don't be so ridiculous!' James starts to thunder.

'Omigod!' Serena exclaims to her husband. 'You did it with someone fat!'

'1980. The Stoat And Badger. Brentford,' Shelley cries. 'You won the bet. A fiver for doing it. A tenner if you could get me to say I loved you.'

'Of course there is one way we can prove it beyond all doubt,' Geraldine smirks, indicating his nether regions.

James falls back in his seat and emits a low squeal of terror. 'My God,' is all he can say. 'My God.'

At this point Alex Cordell decides he'd better do his bit before things get any more out of hand. He rushes from the auditorium up onto the stage. 'Tell him, Serena!' he cries. 'Tell him! Tell him we are lovers! Tell him you are going to leave him for me, Alex Cordell, one of this country's top TV actors soon to be appearing in "The Last Glance", an intriguing murder mystery series on Channel Six, Tuesdays at 10pm.'

Suddenly Shelley's enjoying this. This is lovely. This is just like 'Coombe Ridge Crescent' come real.

Marlon staggers to his feet in bewilderment. 'Serena – is it true? You told me you loved me! And the stars – they told me you were coming for me. They can't be wrong! The stars cannot lie!' he exclaims.

'How can she be in love with you? She's your half-sister,' Alex protests angrily to Marlon.

Gareth leans across to Geraldine. 'He's right, that's too unpleasant,' he mutters. 'It's too much reality, we can't have that.'

'Well what do you want me to do about it now?' she snaps back. 'I told you the plan this morning, you should have said something then!'

'Stop!' comes a shrill voice from the crowd because the traffic jam on the M40 finally got moving again. 'That woman is not her mother. I am her mother!' A resolute figure in a beige twinset comes charging up from the stalls onto the stage. 'I, Barbara Dawlish, am Serena's mother. Serena, tell them I am your mother!' Barbara cries.

'Of course Serena must get this all the time,' says Geraldine to an increasingly perplexed audience. 'People trying to exploit her fame, pretending to be related to her just as this crazy woman is doing now. Serena, would you like me to call security?'

'Look,' says Serena taking her mother by the arm, covering up her mike as Barbara stumbles onto the stage, 'I need to pretend this woman's my mum, just for now,' she whispers into her mother's ear. 'Of course you are my real mum but it's all been arranged by my manager and the producer of the show. It's for my career, to help me get more famous, so I can earn more money and, you know buy a bigger house and a better car.'

Barbara reflects on this a moment. 'Oh, sorry, dear. I hadn't realised that. All right,' she whispers back, 'I'll go and let you get on with it.'

'Thanks, Mum.'

Unfortunately as she utters these last words Serena has removed her hand from the microphone to re-adjust her extensions, a nervous tic of hers, and the audience hears the word Mum and starts to wonder what is going on here. They grope around on their seats to find the remote so they can switch to another channel before they remember this isn't telly, this is something else, something they can't change. This is too much for them to cope with, way too much. They're confused. They've lost the plot. There are too many characters and too much happening all at once without the nice gaps for ads in between each life-altering moment.

Geraldine panics. It was never like this at The Old Vic. She must take control, make order before real life gets in the way of everything and spoils it all. Just in time she remembers the Votercounters and almost swoons with relief.

'So – you've heard their stories. Now it's up to you, the audience, to decide what you think. Is Shelley really Serena's mum? Should James Marlborough acknowledge his love child?'

Meanwhile Gareth nudges Serena on the couch. 'Why didn't you tell me he was so good-looking?' he asks her, gesturing towards Marlon.

'I tried to tell you but you told me he had no hope because he wasn't famous! That he had no promotional potential!'

'His hair's a bit flat but we can easily sort that out. He doesn't have any existing contractual arrangements with any other agent, does he?'

'I told you, Gareth,' Serena says impatiently, 'he's got no work experience at all. All he does is look at stars.'

'Fine. With a face and body as good as his there's no need for him to be able to do anything else anyway.'

'What? So it's OK for me to fancy him?'

'OK? It's bloody obligatory! That boy will make money on TV whatever he does,' Gareth barks as he grabs his ringing mobile.

At this, love suddenly prevails. Serena leaps up and addresses the audience. 'Listen, everyone – I have a confession to make. I have deceived you all. Shelley is not my mother, they just made me pretend she was because they thought my own mother was too boring. I do not love my husband, my marriage has been a joke from the start. I only married him because I thought he'd help me become an actress and anyway I think he's been having it off with Geraldine Fortescue, the producer of this show. I do not love Alex Cordell, that was just a publicity stunt to get everyone to think he isn't gay. Which he is, by the way. My career has been ruined by this programme, people will know that I have lied about my mother just to be famous. But I don't care any more. The man I love is Marlon who by the way isn't my half-brother because Shelley isn't my mother. I was wrong to reject you, Marlon, simply because you are not famous because really I do love you. I will leave James now and be with you, for richer or poorer, because you are the one I love.'

Geraldine is reeling. What the fuck is going on. Has everyone gone insane?

But before she has a chance to stop things and make them turn out differently she realises that the audience have got to their feet and the people are cheering, cheering. Now Serena's rescued them. She's explained everything and made it all nice and simple for them and they're loving all the honesty. Her producer is yelling down her ear – the ratings, the ratings are going through the roof! The advertisers are on the phone – they want to confirm, double, quadruple their media slots for the rest of the series!!

Gareth stands and yells, 'Quiet! Quiet! I have an announcement to make. I've just had a phone call from the head of Channel Six. He's offering Shelley her own prime-time chat show, "Fat and Fabulous", and he's offering Marlon his own astrology forecasting show, "Celebrity Forecasts", and he's offering Serena the starring role in a new drama series, "The Jewel of Gerrards Cross". Shelley! Marlon! Serena! Me! We're all going to be rich! We're all going to be famous! We're all saved!!'

At this the audience go wild, clapping, whooping, screeching in a fevered state of ecstasy. It's still OK to love Serena Dawlish and she's got a nice new boyfriend instead of that old bloke who does poncey theatre no one's interested in anyway! Everything's happy and shiny and nice! They applaud until their hands are sore, and cheer until their throats are raw, but eventually they look at their watches and work out that if they leave now, they'll be home in time to see the first repeat of that day's episode of 'Coombe Ridge Crescent' which they've recorded anyway but what the hell and as one they all leap up and surge out.

Gareth has the contracts in his pocket – he always carries a couple of spares just in case – and signs Marlon and Shelley up there and then.

Then the young lovers, Marlon and Serena, run photogenically from the stage to a waiting car where cameras flash and interviewers ask Marlon what his favourite food is and his favourite TV programme because tomorrow every TV mag in the country will be wanting to know. Marlon says cheese on toast with the edges cut off and everyone scribbles it down. He tries to think about a TV programme but as he hasn't seen anything on television for years apart from the black and white flickers he's stuck for an answer. Fortunately just in time Serena steps in and says, 'It's "Coombe Ridge Crescent" of course!' and everyone laughs and it's all so lovely and all ending so perfectly with handsome Marlon and stunning Serena driving off into the night to consummate their love, now that Marlon knows how it's done.

Meanwhile Gareth and Alex Cordell have exchanged glances and realised that while love is in the air, they may as well go for it and give their own relationship another try. As they are leaving the theatre together Gareth sees Christine Cazale and Holly Diamond running up the steps. 'Where's that slag, that bitch!' they cry in unison. 'Where's she gone? We're gonna tell the world the truth about her, we're going to finish her off!'

'Don't even think about it,' sneers Gareth. 'She's a complete star now, she's more famous than famous! She's famous forever, nothing can touch her any more.'

*

Only Geraldine, Shelley and James are left on stage. James prepares a final soliloquy. 'Geraldine,' he begins, 'I have been a fool. I have neglected you and taken you for granted when I should have cherished and honoured you. I . . .'

'Cut the crap, James,' says Geraldine. 'I'm a TV megastar now! I call the shots. Don't you see? After this evening I simply don't need you any more!' She gathers up her notes and wafts out.

James is left there, with the unfinished speech stuck in his throat.

'There's always me,' comes a small voice from the other end of the sofa.

James turns and looks at Shelley.

'I beg your pardon?'

'What about us?'

'Us? What "us"?'

'Come on. You know that what I said is true. You know Marlon is your son. You know what I said ain't no lie.'

'Ain't no lie?' James repeats slowly.

'Yeah. It ain't. So how about it? You 'n' me?'

'Sorry, my dear, but it's only in plays that things end well. It's only in dramas that the sad, fat one who has led a lonely, empty existence finally gets her reward, that she finds happiness and that justice is seen to be done. This is real life and if you think that I would consider you of all people as a partner well . . . you have no idea,' he snorts.

Shelley stares at him with horror and pain. The secret hopes and dreams of 27 years crack and crumble before her. She stares at him, willing things to be different, wanting magic, needing a miracle. In the end she then stumbles miserably off the stage and disappears.

James is left alone, with no one to look at him or listen to him.

He fumbles nervously in his pocket and finds the card he bought at the petrol station. He reads the words again, the poem about the pain of loneliness, the love for another left abandoned and bereft, the dream of happiness. Bollocks, he thinks. Total bollocks. He screws up the card in his fist.

One of the sound-men clearing up in the wings appears. 'That fat one just gone out, did you hear about her? She's gonna have her own chat show interviewing people who've had difficult lives. She's gonna do well, you can tell. People love an underdog. She's gonna make a packet that one is.'

James reflects.

The man is right. Of course he is.

James needs to ponder for only a moment longer before he realises what he must do and runs off, stage left, into the night.

Recommended Reading

If you enjoyed reading *Defying Reality* and would like to read another book by Karina Mellinger we have published her satire on chic lit, *A Bit Of A Marriage*.

There are other books on our list which should appeal to you if you like the books by Karina Mellinger;

Primordial Soup – Christine Leunens
A Box of Dreams – David Madsen
Androids from Milk – Egner
When the Whistle Blows – Jack Allen
Prayer-Cushions of the Flesh – Robert Irwin
Limits of Vision – Robert Irwin

These can be bought from your local bookshop or online from amazon.co.uk or direct from Dedalus. Please write to **Cash Sales, Dedalus Limited, 24-26, St Judith's Lane, Sawtry, Cambs, PE28 5XE**. For further details of the Dedalus list please go to our website www.dedalusbooks.com or write to us for a catalogue

A Bit Of A Marriage – **Karina Mellinger**

'This arch little novel was published on St Valentine's Day: if you received it as a gift, it might be time to take a long hard look at your relationship. Laura Denver-Barrette, our heroine of sorts, is happily married – and it's unmitigated hell. With malicious, almost masochistic glee, Mellinger describes an avalanche of aggravating details (microwaved chicken lasagne, pots with cherubs on them, a marginally protruding incisor) that would test saints, if they were allowed to marry. With plenty of infidelities and a dying mother in the second-best guest bedroom, this satire on romantic fiction is as delightfully cringe-making and as deliciously embarrassing as Abigail's Party. Perhaps the era of bitch-lit is upon us.'
S.B.Kelly in Scotland on Sunday

'Stress for Laura Denver-Barrette consists of wondering whether to have the dining room done "in a pinky shade of red or a reddy shade of pink", but she has a problem. She loathes her husband David, a boring lawyer who leaves bits of butter in the jam; this is tricky, because it is his money that enables her to live as she does. Laura's ghastly mother (the fortune-telling, Harrods-shopping Lydia) isn't much help, but at least she keeps her mouth shut when she catches David in bed with the Russian cleaner. What will Laura do, apart from flinging herself on a hapless estate agent? This thoroughly jaundiced black comedy is one of those rare books without a single likeable character, and all the better for it.'
Phil Baker in The Sunday Times

'The light and chirpy writing and exaggerated characters are strangely compelling despite their actions. There are some very funny moments too. When making her husband a meal Laura thinks to herself that she "will take extra care to pierce the celophane on the pack of chicken lasagne nicely before she puts it in the microwave". It is a supreme moment of sacrifice for her because "that's the kind of woman she is". The idea that so much can be left to simmer underneath a marriage for years is a provocative one.'

Izzy Kaminiski in The Big Issue

'A satire on chic lit, and a laugh-out loud black comedy. Laura has been married to her rich handsome husband for 15 years but everything he does seems to annoy her. One morning she wakes up and decides she is going to leave him, now all she needs is a reason why. All marriages have their ups and downs, but this marriage is like no other. A must read dark and funny exploration of how wedlock can turn to gridlock.'

JH in Buzz Magazine

'A dark and funny exploration of how wedlock can end in gridlock. Mrs Denver-Barrette, with emphasis on the final "t", a lady of class, charisma and beauty (but only in her own head) has spent another typical Saturday morning drifting in and out of sleep. She's unable to relax and dreads the mess of the kitchen after her husband David has attempted to make breakfast and then played their regular game of push and pull as to whether David will have sex that morning. Nothing much is different, apart from Laura has decided that today she is leaving her husband. Reading further will see David sleeping with the cleaner out of sheer frustration and having an affair with Laura's best friend. But the drama doesn't stop there. Laura seduces David's business partner, while her mother dies in the luxury guest room. All the while she struggles to find a good reason to go. Will Laura leave David or will she find a remedy to cure her allergic reaction to her husband . . .'

HF in The Crack

'David and Laura are in their mid 30s and have been married for 15 years. But theirs is a marriage in tatters. David runs one of the top legal practices in the country with a multi-million pound turnover. Laura on the other hand alternates between half-hearted attempts at being an artist (she has never actually sold a painting) and managing the house – which involves such arduous tasks as choosing a new floral display to correspond with the season, liaising with interior designers to select this year's colour scheme for the dining room and making sure the cleaner Anouschka doesn't forget to polish the silverware. The plot centres upon Laura's dilemma – should she leave her husband? Or more to the point, why should she leave her husband? As Laura puts it: "Leaving him would be easy. Saying why was going to be hard." Fidelity is not of particular importance to either David or Laura. In the course of a few months, David gets Anouschka pregnant and has an affair with Laura's best friend, Louella, while Laura has sex with a young estate agent (who confusingly is also called David). Written in the third person, the narrative perspective regularly switches between the main characters allowing the reader greater insight into each of the characters, from Anouschka's unthinking adoration of "Meester David" to Laura's habitual tantrums whenever anyone dares to defy her. A more aristocratic and lighter version of Nick Hornby's *How To Be Good*, *A Bit Of A Marriage* satirises the frivolity of Laura's upper class way of life throughout: "Her only commitments are to organise the house, manage the social diary (and) keep herself looking slim and better looking than anyone else David is likely to meet." A worthwhile read for any woman who has ever contemplated divorce but thought they might miss the Bentley.'

Kate Fleming in Big Issue in the North

'CHICK LIT is a much derided genre, yet its snazzily packaged offspring nestle comfortably at the top of the charts.

People accuse these books of being tired and formulaic. But here is a new contender on the scene: Karina Mellinger works within and subverts that formula to depict the myriad nuances of marital breakdown, and achieves something well sculpted, sharply written and biting amusing. The more Mellinger reveals, the more we feel a strange mixture of pity and contempt for these characters trapped in their weaknesses. Laura's ten-point plan to marry David is one of the funniest and saddest things I have read in a while. This is a dark, toothy, elegant winner.'

Philip Womack in The Literary Review

£9.99   ISBN 978 1 903517 46 8   226p   B. Format